REVENGE IS SWEET, WITCH

BETTINA M JOHNSON

AQUA RAVEN PUBLISHING

Revenge is Sweet, Witch

ISBN: 978-1-7350692-7-2 (paperback)

Cover art by StunningBookCovers.com

CHAPTER 1

"Why isn't she waking up?"

I fussed with the coverlet, tucking it around my mother, Adelaide Croy Sweet, to ward off the chill, even though our temperatures here in Sweet Briar, Georgia, had been steadily improving. I was amazed to see daffodils and forsythia making an appearance in my garden —something that would not be happening in the Catskill Mountains of New York State, where I lived most of my life —for another two months, if then.

I'd just recently found out the woman who was in a perpetual slumber in her old bedroom in the house I had inherited was, in fact, my mother and not my aunt. It was a very long and sordid tale involving evil witches, my parents, and my aunt concealing the structure of their relationship and the verity behind my birth, along with so many unanswered questions which resulted in murder, mayhem, and a mystery I had yet to solve.

Trying to help me solve this puzzle was my great-grandmother, Adriana Dolce, my father Charlie's grandmother, our family's matriarch, and a formidable dark witch. Don't let the fact that she is a centenarian fool you—Granny is a hellion in a cape and pointy hat, a dark witch like me, and the average Joe would be crazy to cross her path with anything but the utmost respect.

Oh, yes, witches. We were a rather large and prolific family—the Dolces and Croys—just to name a few of the surnames that made up my crazy clan. Some of that mayhem I mentioned could very well be our fault. Using spells and magic always came with a price, as I just recently found out.

My name is Lily Sweet, one of the aforementioned dark witches, and no—I do not do evil things. It's more like I am one asshat away from letting my magic loose and protecting the innocent or seeking justice for those wronged.

I'm a Sweet, not a Dolce, because my grandfather changed his name, much to the disappointment of both his parents. My dad, Charlie, preferred Sweet as well, so there you have it.

"That is what the Clerics are trying to figure out, Liliana. That and why she went under so deeply in the first place." Adriana, keen on getting to the bottom of this family's afflictions and hellbent on taking on the matter of one, Donna Fredricks, grumbled in reply. Granny wanted to throttle Donna until she spilled all the secrets that she'd been keeping from us.

I wanted to throttle her because of all the vile things she'd done my family.

I was beyond frustrated and impatient. When I first freed my mother from her sentence of being bound to my cat Wicked—a nasty spell had them fused for the last twenty-one years with Adelaide stuck inside my cat—I was sure my mother would have all the answers to the questions that had been haunting my family for years. And thought, great, now we will learn everything!

But, yet again, I had to learn to be patient, seeing as how

she had been sleeping now going on two and a half weeks with only the occasional eye flutterings and brief smile to let us know she wasn't in any dire predicaments. While it was unusual for a patient to be out so long, the witch Clerics informed us that the extraordinary circumstances around Adelaide's decades-long furry prison could be the reason for such a lengthy recuperation.

"Just try to be patient, cara. Adelaide will come around when she can. She knows we need those answers."

That was all well and good. However, I wasn't a very patient person.

"Plus, we have to attend to other pressing matters. I want to hit that lower level of the prison, despite Mortimer's dire warnings, before the Witch Council decides to grow a backbone and blows the place to smithereens!"

Mortimer Snodgrass was a vampire who aided us in recent weeks. Despite any preconceived notions you may carry regarding the bloodsuckers, old Morty was a good egg, even if he did warn us not to enter the witch prison.

Wait a minute. We were what?

"WHEN DID you plan on enlightening me on this bit of news? Or was I to be left in the dark until the day of the attack?"

"Who said we weren't heading there today?" Adriana sniffed.

My eyes widened to epic proportions. We were back downstairs, relieved of watching over Adelaide by a nurse the Clerics assigned. I was chasing after my great-grand-mother for an explanation when her words stopped me short. I squinted suspiciously at the old menace. There was no way Adriana would thrust me in the middle of a witch war against Donna without some plan in place and be prepared to the hilt. Right?

"Oh, stop looking so alarmed. I just want to brainstorm and discuss some ideas I have flitting around in my mind, test the waters, so to speak, before we make a run on the prison. I called your partners in crime over. They will be here shortly," said Adriana primly, then went over to examine Wicked, who was sunning herself on the windowsill in my dining room. "How has she been since the spell reversal? Any signs of distress or malaise?"

"None that I can see," I replied, giving my magical furball a fond look. I joined my great-grandmother near her resting spot. Wicked was now watching us surreptitiously with green eyes open to mere slits. I don't think she appreciated the scrutiny.

"So, who is coming? I should put a pot of coffee on."

"Me for one." Lorcan Reid, the town of Sweet Briar's yummy mechanic, my landlord of sorts, and current—and hopefully, last—boyfriend, just walked in holding a box from my Uncle Stephen's café. This meant one thing and one thing only.

"Pastries?" I squeaked, hopefully.

"Pastries," Lorcan replied, nodding his head in the affirmative.

I squealed and rushed over, grabbing the box out of his hands, and placed it on the dining room table. When I took a peek inside the box, I swooned.

"I wish I gave you that kind of reaction. It almost makes me want to turn into a giant cannoli," grumped Lorcan. Then he chuckled when I gave him a peck on his cheek. The sparkle lighting his gorgeous brown eyes had me melting a bit more.

"I can make that happen." Adriana offered with a dark chuckle.

We chose to ignore her.

"Here, sit, I am going to get the coffee on and... oh! Look what I can do!"

With that, I focused my magic, calling it up and out of me, and pointed my hand toward the taper candles lining my long table. "I've been practicing my basic witch stuff...see?"

I uttered a soft, "Flame." command.

I finally mastered lighting candles without burning down the town—or my home and watched with joy as the wicks lit and the flames began gently dancing, giving the room a nice warm glow.

Lorcan came over to me, giving me a quick hug, and mumbled in my ear, "There is nothing basic witch about you."

Giggling, I took a moment to enjoy being in Lorcan's arms. But then I glanced over at Adriana a bit self-consciously since we hadn't yet announced our standing, and I worried Lorcan might still be hesitant to have our families know we were an item.

"Oh, pulease! Quit your fretting. You two have been making moony eyes at each other since the Edith fiasco. You weren't fooling me." The great-grandmother informed us both.

Finally, having embraced being a dark witch, I threw myself into my studies with gusto. Daily dedication to practice and spell crafting had made me rather proficient at some magic—my unique talents. The basic stuff, however, I was finding more challenging to master.

My advanced spells, unique to me, seemed to flow naturally. I guess, in a way, it made sense. I wasn't around Sweet Briar and my family as a little witchling, learning from an example like a child who grew up with their family would. Instead, I had to learn the mundane in my mid-twenties, and it certainly has been interesting. The advanced magic came more quickly—it just clicked.

"Tell me about it. It's enough to make me gag. All this kissing and touching."

"Edith!" I cried out, startled by my ghostly visitor. While I was finally getting used to the idea that the ghost of Edith Plank, the former town librarian, one-time enemy, and murder victim, had decided to stay on and haunt me, I was not too fond of the way she'd manifest without warning.

"Can't you make some signal or noise before you pop in to announce your arrival?"

"What...like an alarm? A horn is supposed to be less startling than my voice?" She harumphed.

"Well, we need to come up with something—or you are going to give me a heart attack someday."

Adriana was looking over my shoulder, and I'd noted her eyes go round. "Um, Liliana, did you focus all your energy forward when you lit those candles?"

"I... why? I think? What's wrong?" I asked with some trepidation.

"Oh, nothing, except the dish towel in your kitchen just went up in flames."

Ack!

Groaning a little, I spun around just in time to see the last of the flames die down, leaving a smoldering mess in its wake. Perfect. And in front of Lorcan, too. *Grr.*

Edith was howling and clutching at her sides, which turned to hiccupping, her shoulders shaking in merriment. Who knew a ghost could get the hiccups? She laughed so hard she reached out to lean against the dining room wall but fell through and wound up in the living room. I was not amused.

I stomped into the kitchen and continued into the mudroom, grabbing the dustpan and broom.

"Here. Give me the pala, and you make your coffee. I can do that." Adriana held her hand out.

"Pala?" I scrunched up my face in confusion.

"Pala! The dustpan. Pala means little shovel in some Italian dialects. Really, cara, you must learn some of the language."

Handing the item in question over to Adriana, I proceeded to get the coffee going and began gathering mugs.

"Who else will be here?" I asked.

"Jake and Becky, Andrea too," Lorcan replied, grabbing a wet sponge to wipe off the counter, removing the last of the ash.

"So, the usual," I stated and got enough mugs down, placing them on my new kitchen table. I say new, but my parents had this very table when I was a little girl. It was a gorgeous piece that had been living in my great-grandfather Antonio's workshop. He had removed it and the six chairs that went with it to maintain its luster with oils, preserving the piece rather than leave it here when the home was empty for so many years. Now, back in its rightful place, I had been enjoying my morning cup of coffee, sitting and staring out into the backyard looking for more signs of spring.

We all heard the crunch of gravel, but it wasn't my friends and cousin who walked in the backdoor a few minutes later, but my Aunt Iona, Adelaide's sister.

"I know you are probably sick of seeing my face, Lily, but I thought I'd sit with Addy a spell and read to her. You never know what may help her come back to us and decide it's time to awaken."

Out of everyone who was delighted to have Adelaide back in their lives, none was more excited and grateful than her big sister, Iona, who had come over daily ever since we brought Addy home. We decided here in her old home after being assured by the Clerics that she could rest and restore her health in no better place. Once she was looked over at the hospital and cleared medically, that is. The nurse was staying with us most of the day, and between she and Iona, my mother had the utmost in care.

As I mentioned, Adelaide was married to my father. However, this was not common knowledge, even among the Witch Council in our town and the Elders. My family and I kept that bit of news under wraps until we could figure out who was an enemy and who we could trust. Everyone in this gossipy village was already fully aware of the fantastic turn of events that Addy had been imprisoned in Wicked the cat by nefarious means. However, most everyone still believed my parents were Jessica, Adelaide's older sister, and my father, Charlie. The only ones who knew the secret were those closest to me: My great-grandparents Antonio and Adriana, their daughter; my Aunt Chiara and her husband, my Uncle Stephen and their children Steve Junior and Andrea. My Aunt Iona, the eldest of the three Croy sisters who was married to my Uncle Owen Haywood, Judge Haywood, another Elder. His sister June, best friend to Jessica and friendly with Charlie and Adelaide when they were all children. June was married to Dennis Carter, and their son Jake, an attorney, and his girlfriend and bookshop owner, Becky Dolan, who were some of my besties, were in on the secret. Lorcan's parents, Eileen and Henry Reid as well.

The last four to know were Susanne Washington, our family friend. She was the gatekeeper to the forbidden areas of the library and Keeper of Tomes. Susanne also sang in her church choir—yeah, go figure. Her niece, Keisha, my friend, and Grandpa Antonio's trusted full-time nurse. The others were Olivia Odgen-Meyers, an Elder and contemporary of my great-grandmother, and her grandnephew, Detective Brian Chase—both powerful Veritums or truth seekers.

My Aunt Iona and Uncle Owen chose not to tell their son, my cousin Doug, nor their estranged daughter, my cousin Nora, of this tidbit. Doug, because he would probably forget and mention it in passing to the wrong people. Not because he was deceitful, but that was just his way. Nora? Nora and I had a tenuous relationship that had quickly deteriorated upon my return to Sweet Briar, Georgia, and I had no intention of trusting her, despite her aid a few weeks back now. We just could not entrust her with this information—her past transgressions too harsh to easily forgive.

I had many other close family and friends. My circle seemed to keep growing, but no one else knew the secret of Adelaide and Charlie. Hiding the fact that it was they who had married, and not he and Jessica, who I thought was my mother my entire life until she passed from cancer this past summer, is an ongoing puzzle. The need for deception was the topic of conversation and the first thing Andrea asked when she waltzed into the kitchen with Jake and Becky on her heels.

"Hail, hail, the gang's all here!" She smiled as she made that remark, then observed the box of pastries from her dad's café and winked at Lorcan. "I see you stopped and picked up some goodies!"

"You know I can't resist your dad's offerings! And I knew how bereft Lily would be without a cannoli...or ten."

Hey!

"Coffee and pastries! What could be better?" Jake asked no one in particular.

"The love of a good woman?" said Becky and gave him a poke in the ribs as she scooted by, taking a seat at the table. "Although, I could do with a cannoli, myself." She squealed as he tickled her ribs in passing.

I sat across from her after setting the pot of coffee down and turned to Adriana.

"Are we discussing the mystery around Charlie, Addy, and Jess?" Andrea queried while pouring herself a cup and looking at me. I shrugged and turned to Adriana.

"OK, the floor is yours. What's on the agenda for this little gathering?"

"What's on the agenda is coming up with a plan of attack regarding Donna Fredricks and figuring out how to get you back to the lower level of the Forbidden Library."

"Oh. That's a great place to start. And... hold on, what?"

And here I thought we'd only talk about breaking into the prison—which was bad enough. But it seems my great-grandmother had something else up her sleeve.

CHAPTER 2

"*Y*ou are not sending me back down there."

"But I am."

"No. You are not. And this time, I know you need approval from the Elders to get in there."

"But I am, despite that."

"No, you are not."

"I am."

"Not! Don't think for one second that I am going to head back to the library, hit the bathroom stall, and traverse that three flipping miles, let alone having you slice my hand open and slather my blood on a demons tongue guardian pervert. I won't do it. Even if I'd like to visit my Jerry Godfather, I refuse. I won't."

"Will." Adriana smiled serenely.

"I will not. And you can't make me." I pounded my fist on the table, making the cups, and my friends, jump a little.

"Yes, I am."

Argh!

"Listen, you old troublemaker. You will not subject me to your reprehensible plans without fully knowing what I am doing and why. What is so important that I risk life and limb having to face those repugnant Sentinels again and... and... No. I just won't do it."

"And yet, you will."

"You are so sure of yourself, aren't you?" I screeched, making Lorcan, Jake, Andrea, and Becky back away from the table slightly, with similar looks of alarm on their faces.

"You, crazy, maniacal, bats-in-the-belfry, old witch."

"I am," Adriana replied, fussing with the hem of her shirt, then smoothing her hands down across the front before placing them on her lap. She looked up and smiled, wickedly, at me. "You see? I've discovered that there is something down there you want more than anything in this world."

"And what would that be, you crazy dingbat?"

"Answers. All of the answers."

Well, how do you like that? It looks like I am going back to the Forbidden Library. Isn't that just great?

"OK, no more riddles. No more cryptic messages. No more bull. Spill it. What do you know, and how did you find it out? More importantly, who told you the answers were in the forbidden library section, and when?"

I crossed my arms and sat back, pouting.

"Answers to what, exactly?" Lorcan asked.

My friends had been looking back and forth between Adriana and me as if they were at a tennis match. Before my great-grandmother could respond, Aunt Iona came back down the stairs—a serving tray in her hand. "That lovely nurse is heading out now, so I am going to make more tea and continue reading to Addy. I'll get out of your way, but I might steal something from that delicious box on the table!"

Iona bustled through the dining room, heading to the kitchen, and we all noted as the nurse came down the stairs waving goodbye before she slipped out the front door, closing it softly behind her.

All eyes turned back to Adriana, and I swear she was enjoying keeping us in suspense—the demented dingbat. Forget that we were so much alike; any fool could see I'd probably grow to be just as evil and mischievous, which explained why we fought so often. I didn't have to like it, though. Accept it was a given. Like it? Nope.

"Talk."

Adriana reached under the table and retrieved a box she'd had at her feet. Taking the items out one at a time, she carefully laid them on the table until the box was empty. Lined up in a row was the dagger I'd discovered that belonged to Adelaide, a tiny poppet that represented my father in some way, and the little figurine of a black cat with green eyes that I used to become invisible and hide from the Sentinels in the forbidden levels of the library. Somehow it wound up with me when I was whisked out of the library with Lorcan and my mother—thanks to Mortimer.

Also laid out was one of the photos I had brought down with me from New York State, of Adelaide holding me.

The last was a new item I didn't recognize. However, it tickled at my memory as something I might have seen but forgotten. If I had to describe the item or what it did, I'd be at a loss for words. It was carved wood with an intricate pattern; I thought I saw palm trees and flowers and a water feature etched in the wood. I couldn't figure out what the item was, however. A cylinder of some sort with glass at either end. A wooden container to hold something in its core, maybe. The last item was a silver inlaid square box about the size a Big Mac comes in... but just a tad taller.

"Liliana. In consulting with Olivia, we have been going back and forth with her involvement with Edith and their attempts to find answers in the Forbidden Library. I've decided Olivia has no hidden agenda and is firmly on our side—despite her use of Edith."

"She didn't use me! I willingly helped Olivia." Edith spoke up then, looking offended. I'd almost forgotten she was among us and that she also knew of my parent's deception. That meant my dearly departed Aunt Moira, the other ghost flitting about my home, also would see this fact.

I opened my mouth to respond, but Adriana cut me off before I could get a word out.

"Oh, hush, Spooky. You know perfectly well you were on the wrong team when you were among the living."

Lorcan, Jake, Andrea, and Becky began looking around the room. They were well aware that Adriana and I could see and hear ghosts. But it still gave them the willies.

"And what team was that?" Edith inquired a bit haughtily.

"Team *Take Down the Dolce Clan*, headed by none other than Wilhelmina Dietrich, your grandmother! Along with those ancient families too dense to see, their futile attempts at insurrection will bring them endless frustration and constipation."

"Wait, the frustration I get," I ventured, "what does constipation have to do with anything?" I asked.

"Oh, I add on a monthly spell that binds anyone in town who even remotely speaks ill of our family. It gets triggered whenever anyone starts whispering rumors about us or casts aspersions and makes it difficult for them to stay regular."

"Nice." I raised my eyebrows and nodded in approval at such deviousness.

"Indeed."

"That explains my family and their usual constitution," mumbled Edith.

"Yes, it does." I agreed with her assessment; that family is tightly wound. I turned to Adriana, "you have all the best spells."

"You have quite the arsenal yourself, cara." She replied, eyes twinkling.

"We be bad witches!"

We bumped fists, and Jake shook his head at us.

"You two are at each other's throats, and then in an instant, you are in a mutual admiration society. I can't keep up!" crying out, Jake made the two of us chuckle at his frustration.

Not cackle, though. I don't cackle. *Yet.*

"Wait. If it's that easy to do, this constipation spell, why can't you cast something like that, or stronger, on enemies? Wouldn't that prevent all attacks?" Andrea asked.

"My darling great-granddaughter, you ask a smart question, but keep thinking on your query and tell me why it wouldn't be possible."

Andrea, forehead wrinkled in consternation, pondered just a moment before her face cleared, and she replied, "dark magic. It would take vast amounts to maintain such a spell and magic always..."

"...comes with a price," I grumbled, finishing for Andrea. I'd learned that firsthand after my initial foray into the Forbidden Library.

"Brava. There would involve too many repercussions in so vast a spell."

Lorcan cleared his throat and looked pointedly at Adriana. "Not that I mind going off on a tangent, but you were saying...Olivia and consulting with her? What did you discover?"

"The cabinet. The one Edith hid in that first time she ventured down to the lowest level, and the Sentinels could not find her. In that cupboard is a key left by Charles that will open this little silver trinket box. I do not know when he placed it in that cupboard, but Olivia informed me she had put Edith under a spell without her knowledge, so she'd remember all the items and listed them when in a trance. Edith was never aware that she gave out this information."

Edith did indeed look shocked at this news, but for once, remained quiet.

"It seems my grandson left this key in the lower level. Then he gathered the silver box and a note to go with it and mailed them to Olivia one week after he'd disappeared. He left instructions to open that cupboard should anyone in his family break the seal on the library side and enter the forbidden levels.

When Olivia found out about your successful entry, even with the temporary loss of her grand-nephew, Brian, she knew it was time to retrieve that key. It is hidden in the cupboard, but only the heir who entered the long way can use the Oculus Rod to find it. That was another reason why he put the seal on one side. It triggered the item to appear. Only we knew nothing of this until Olivia showed me the note."

"Oculus Rod? What on earth is that?" Lorcan asked curiously.

"This is the Oculus Rod." Adriana used her index finger and pushed the wooden item forward a few inches.

"It looks like a kaleidoscope," Becky stated.

"It does, a bit...but when you look into it, it will reveal the truth in some way...though what that truth is, I do not know. Moreover, what we are supposed to use it on, is still a mystery, although I suspect it is the contents in the cupboard. That key is essential because a key to a locked box usually means some kind of answer is inside, no?"

"So even though Edith managed to get to that level hide in the cupboard but not knowing all she was looking at...somehow she spied a key?" I asked, "it doesn't make any sense. She told us she saw all manner of things but could not begin to describe them. How did she know she was looking at a key?" I gazed at Edith, eyebrows raised.

Edith began nodding her head in agreement. "Lily is

right. I don't remember any key. I saw unbelievable items, but I would remember a key, I would think!"

"Perhaps the cabinet is charmed, and only under a trance can you reveal what you saw. Perhaps the subconscious recalls the key. We won't know until you go to the forbidden levels and find out," proclaimed Adriana.

Well great.

"Plus, I have one more reason I need you to go to the forbidden levels," Adriana stated primly.

Why did I not like the sound of this?

"Pray-tell. What next?" I asked, jutting my chin out in another pout.

"Well...speaking of good old Morty...we kind of need to find him. In his rush to head back into his delightful slumber, he managed to lose his cell phone on the outside of the lower levels when he closed it off, sealing himself inside. I need him for this run on the prison I want to carry out. You need to find him, wake him up, and bring him to me."

I sat there with my mouth hanging open yet again, a common occurrence when dealing with Adriana.

"You told me Mortimer could take on any form, being part shifter. What am I supposed to do? Run around the lower levels, dodging the Sentinels and tap on every chair or wall sconce until he rouses?"

"In a word? Yes."

"Why am I the one who needs to do this? Can't you go down there? And don't hit me with the 'I'm old and feeble' line...you were the one who told me you planned on taking up spelunking...well...go spelunk then!"

It was Adriana's turn to sit back and pout as she stared at me unblinking. Then a chilling smile spread across her face, and I knew she was about to drop the final bombshell on me.

"The key is exactly like the entry requirement to the Forbidden Library that Charles set up. Only his heir going

17

downwards can retrieve it. You are his only heir, so you are the only one who can bring it to the surface. The Oculus Rod was a gift from Charles to you when you were a baby. See this photo of you and Adelaide? Look at what you are clutching in your hand like a rattle. It's the rod."

I definitely had a bone to pick with my father when and if we ever managed to find him and bring him home.

CHAPTER 3

"*I* can't believe I'm doing this again. I really can't believe I'm doing this again. Why am I doing this to myself? I could run away. Head back to New York, live in blissful ignorance of anything remotely witch. I could pretend I never heard of Sweet Briar, Georgia, or the Dolce clan. I... "

"You'd miss me," Lorcan stated.

There is that.

We spent the rest of the evening discussing theories on the dagger and the poppet doll and why Adelaide was still out of it. Nothing we came up with seemed to make sense, and we parted, frustrated but determined to get to the bottom of it. Everyone was resigned to the fact that we'd have to get to Donna Fredricks before the Elders and their bureaucratic red tape and utilitarian ways did something stupid and got to her before we did. Therefore, we needed Mortimer's aid. Even I grudgingly admitted there was no other choice but to find and wake him once more. It didn't mean I would like it.

One of the main reasons I was in full-on dissent mode

was not entering the library's lower levels via the basement of the church Susanne Washington was a member of because I had to use the main entrance. So much for being Gatekeeper and Keeper of Tomes. Lorcan and I had just left her congregation, where Susanne had informed us the door had been damaged and was unstable. She had been cleaning out her area of the Forbidden Library, fussing over a wee book no bigger than a Cheez-It cracker that she couldn't recall ever having seen before. The writing was impossible to make out, but she couldn't just chuck it into a pile and forget about it. Fussing over books was her job! To know each tome and what it did or said.

"Ah well, I guess I'll be sticking it in my purse until I can find some time to research it a bit more." We watched as she placed the book in her purse, and I became impatient because I needed to find my vampire! The lower level was unstable due to Mortimer's tumultuous rescue attempts while trying to recover Brian Chase.

Brian fell into an abyss.

To make a long story short, his evil girlfriend, Yolanda Seranno, tried to kill me along with Brian, Lorcan, and Adelaide. I managed to do her in, but not before Brian fell into the trap she had set. If it wasn't for Mortimer saving the day, I don't know if Lorcan and I, along with Adelaide and my cat, Wicked, would have ever left the Forbidden Library alive. Imagine my horror when I discovered not only was Yolanda Donna Fredricks's niece, we were all related. Yeah. I'm still grappling with that revelation.

Brian was still on the mend from his ordeal. While I am thrilled he made it back to us, I still felt awkward about our past relationship. Not that we'd ever been anything more than a few pleasant dates and some minor necking. Unless you asked Brian, who insisted we were destined to make tiny witchlings of our own and ride off into the sunset on our broomsticks. I had decided early on that his type was not my type, and in my naivety and awkwardness around men, I had more of an infatuation going.

Brian was incredibly gorgeous; black hair and sea-blue eyes. Despite trying to break things off and remain on friendly terms, he'd occasionally overstep my boundaries and held on to a slim hope that I'd come around to his dream of us being together forever. That was one of his only downfalls; he was arrogant and pushy.

It wasn't going to happen. I fell hard and fast for Lorcan Reid and had no intention of ruining our chances of a happily-ever-after.

Because of the church entry being out of commission, I'd have to resort to what Adriana and I had done a few weeks ago. I'd have to take the long way in via our town's library, in through the employee bathroom, into a stall, and down the long three-mile trek to reach the room where Jerry, my fairy-godfather, resided. I'd have to ask him if there was another way into the lower level and pray he'd let me in. Jerry guarded the doorway blocked from his side, but Adriana informed us there must be several more paths down. Jerry could come and go at will, and he had disappeared mysteriously the last time we were in his realm. This meant he knew of another way. Hence my complaining.

I hated that walk.

But before I'd make that horrible journey, I had an idea to try out.

Lorcan and I were now standing in the spot down the hill from Susanne's Methodist Church where Mortimer had sealed the temporary entrance to the Forbidden Library. He blasted a hole in a cliff in his rescue attempt then closed it once he'd found Brian. I was taking a chance that the very wall I was contemplating might be Mortimer in hiding. You see, the first time we crossed paths with the friendly vampire, who was also a shifter, he looked like a giant rock formation that was really a secret entrance to the witch prison.

Yeah. I know. Fantastical is my world.

"What should I do? Knock on it? Press my hand up against it and call to him?" I asked, biting my lower lip nervously. Lorcan, running his hand across his chin, frowned while pondering my question.

"Maybe push on the stone? Would he even feel us touching him if he were deeply asleep?" Lorcan responded.

"I considered bringing some silver with us and tossing it at the wall," I informed Lorcan. We had awoken the giant vampire after Adriana tossed one of Andrea's silver earrings through the locked gate of the hidden prison entrance, which caused Mortimer some minor pain. I was hesitant to repeat the process because while approachable... yeah, vampire!

What if he had a limited amount of patience dealing with burned flesh he'd needed to regenerate every time someone chucked silver in his direction? I didn't want to find out the hard way he'd hold a grudge. Or decide I'd be a tasty snack.

I didn't want to be a vampire lollipop.

"Let's try tapping lightly and calling out to him. Adelaide isn't waking up, and the Clerics are starting to worry. I have a feeling we are running out of time and options. What if finding the key and opening the box wakes her up?" A long shot, I know, but I was desperate.

I carefully placed my hands on the stone façade and began tapping and gently pushing while calling out to Mortimer. Lorcan walked over to my left and did the same.

Nothing.

We kept at it for another fifteen minutes getting louder and using our palms to tap with more force. Still, nothing happened other than an angry squirrel chattering at us in annoyance for disturbing his peaceful nut gathering.

"I guess I am doing this the hard way," I stated despairingly.

"Well, I will be right there with you, and Jake, Andrea, and Becky plan on joining us. I'm sure your granny will be along if for nothing but to torture us with dire predictions and warnings of the Sentinels and their eating habits or some such. You won't be unaccompanied."

This time.

In truth, my friends were with me last time, Lorcan and Brian that is, and look what had happened. Not only did we magically get separated, with Yolanda plotting and planning our demise, both of my 'protectors' wound up imprisoned. I didn't intend to repeat the possibility of anything going wrong and losing them again. Yet, I didn't dare to inform Lorcan of my intent to head down unaccompanied. Adriana intended I go on my expedition to find Mortimer and recover the key tomorrow. I had other plans. I would sneak out tonight without anyone the wiser.

This was *my* task, and mine alone.

* * *

LATER THAT EVENING, I checked in on my mother and her nurse, making sure nothing had changed in the last thirty minutes since I'd last looked in. Nothing had. Adelaide remained in a peaceful slumber that seemed deeper than the previous four times I checked—her gorgeous red hair fanned out on the pillow, eyes closed and breathing normally. Upon closer inspection, I noted a slight frown marring her usually pleasant appearance, giving her a harried look as if she had a bad dream. This made me nervous. The nurse tried not to show her concern, but even I knew this wasn't normal.

Time was of the essence. I somehow felt that everything was tied to the key and the little silver box that remained on the dining room table, waiting to be opened. I crept down the stairs and walked over to it now. Beside it sat the Oculus Rod. Picking it up, I peered into the one side where the eyepiece was and found myself staring at a typical kaleidoscope. Beautiful, intricate patterns graced the lens as I pointed it toward a light source. It was nothing special. It was a lovely piece, but still just a kaleidoscope from all outward appearances. Slipping it in my pocket, I spied the dagger and the poppet, along with the photo of Adelaide and me.

Sighing with frustration, I wondered at the puzzles that seemed to escalate with every twist and turn in my family drama. I knew opening the silver box might hold the component we needed to put it all together, which made me all the more determined to head out shortly.

I wandered into the kitchen and found Wicked, my cat, lapping at her water bowl. She paused to give me a squinty look then continued drinking. Despite our love-hate relationship, I was thrilled she remained a healthy cat, even though she must be over twenty years old. Being a furry magical being had sustained her youthfulness far past like what any typical cat would be.

"I'm glad you can't squeal on me, cat. I need to do this by myself and not risk my friends doing something I alone am supposed to do. It's not fair to them, despite the arguments they'd have at the ready."

I gave Wicked a pat and prepared to head out the door, but before I could, a voice called out to me.

"Where be the spòrs this night? Are ye goin' on a randan? Is it wise tae go off on yer own, lass?"

I jumped at the voice and spun around to find the ghost of my great aunt smiling benignly at me. Moira Muir Fortune was my Scottish aunt, younger sister of my grandmother, Maggie. Moira died after a spell she concocted went horribly wrong, and now she seemed to enjoy haunting me along with Edith Plank.

I lived a charmed life...not.

It's not that I minded having the two ghosts in my life. I just wished they came with an alarm to warn me of their imminent arrival and give me a thirty-minute heads up! Getting naked around here had me peering over my shoulder, expecting an audience. It was getting old fast!

"Aunt Moira! I didn't see you sitting there." In actuality, I wasn't sure if she was sitting, standing, or doing a jig. All I could see was her shoulders and head. The rest of her was wispy smoke. "Spòrs? Randan?" I asked.

"Fun! A rowdy spree, lass. Although methinks yer off on yer own!"

"I don't want anyone to get hurt. Those Sentinels are no joke, and after what happened last time, my conscience can't handle risking anyone else. This is my problem. My parents. My puzzle to solve and task to accomplish."

"Dae ye have no one tae be takin' then? What aboot this fine lassie here? Both of ye need a bit' o scran in ye then ye kin be on yea way, no? She's a fine companion she is!"

Scran? Oh! Food. And I guessed my aunt suggested I take Wicked again. Although last time she managed to show up just as we were preparing to enter the lower levels. Freaky cat.

"I don't know, Auntie. She did help me last time, and I am very grateful for that, but I don't want to worry about her while I am dealing with those Sentinels again!"

"Noo jist haud on, lass. Ye might need this wee bairn along with ye. Och, aye agree with ye, but Wicked might help ye keep the heid. No journey is worth goin' alone. I dinnae ken what ye be up against, but she can be yer eyes and ears. A bit o' comfort in the dark."

I looked down at Wicked, who didn't give me much of a

choice when she suddenly strolled over to the back door, jumped up to twist the knob, and crept out into the yard, tail swishing behind her.

Great.

I grabbed a bag of black jellybeans and ran after my cat calling out to Moira. "If Edith shows up, don't tell her what I'm doing. She will blab to Adriana, and that won't end well."

For me anyway.

"Whit's fur ye'll no go by ye! What's meant tae happen will happen. Haste Ye Back!"

I will certainly try, that's for sure!

CHAPTER 4

*G*etting into the library was no problem. I arrived ten minutes before my friend and the new head librarian, Martha Mosley, was preparing to close for the night. I was used to her routine and knew she would scour the aisles looking for stragglers then check the bathrooms before locking the front door. Then she'd head to the back rooms where the employee area was located and spend a few minutes ensuring everything was in order before locking up and leaving by the back door.

I just had to find someplace to hide where she wouldn't look, so I could sneak into the employee bathroom where the entrance to the lower level was.

I almost wished I'd asked my cousin, Andrea, to accompany me—Andrea was gifted at cloaking spells and could have made us both disappear. I was kind of jealous that I couldn't learn this for myself as it was one of the unique witchy talents she possessed. Oh, there were plenty of cloaking spells out there, but Andrea's raw talent could not be equaled by many. Even if I managed to cloak myself with a potion, it wouldn't last as long as hers—or be as strong.

However, I could have used it now, so I made a note to practice a few. Somehow, I suspected there would be more sneaking around in my future!

Staying undetected was made equally tricky by the fact I was clutching Wicked to my chest and trying to keep her quiet—she was not happy with the situation and let me know it by digging her claws into my flesh. As luck would have it, Martha hadn't noticed me arrive, and I hid behind a shelf and watched her lock the front door, then she went into the public bathroom.

Ducking down in a crouching position, I crept into the children's area and hid behind one of the big comfy sofas near the wall. I whispered an agitated "hush" to Wicked, who was not impressed. I'm convinced she had managed to draw blood.

I gave her a tight-lipped glare; she just flattened her ears, tail lashing, eyes wild.

Martha came out of the restroom and made her rounds, straightening books and dusting as she went. This took about ten minutes. Switching off the lights, she rechecked the front door, making sure all was secure. Then she went into the employee area. I breathed a sigh of relief and knew I would just have to wait until I heard her arm the security system then leave out the back, locking the door behind her. While the alarm beeped, I'd have just enough time to dash to the break-room before the sensors kicked on.

How Wicked and I would manage to leave the library was another matter, and one I'd worry about when we returned... *if* we returned.

I could hear thunder rumbling in the distance. Spring in Georgia came early. Way early. Like February early, and with it came storms. In the first days of March, I couldn't believe how many tornado warnings were issued daily for most of the state. So far, up here in the mountains, it had just been severe thunderstorm warnings, but one never knew when a nasty storm could turn into something worse.

Suddenly, I heard the steady beep of the alarm and a solid click of the door shutting and knew it was time to dash to the employee area.

Securing a protesting Wicked, I tore around the sofa, through the children's section, across the central part of the library, and flew into the employee bathroom, where I skidded to a halt and screamed like a teenaged girl in a horror flick. My shrieking caused Wicked to poof and hiss as she squirmed out of my arms and scrambled down my back. The reason I screamed was standing in front of the bathroom stall; all ninety-eight pounds soaking wet of her.

"You! What the heck are you doing here?" I screeched as I came face to face with my great-grandmother, Adriana.

"The same thing as you...only I am along for the ride...or walk, as it is. You'd have to get up pretty early to outsmart me, Squirt." She sniffed.

"But how... when... I don't... how did you know I was planning on doing this tonight?"

"You're Adelaide's daughter."

"But that doesn't explain anything," I protested.

"It does to me. If you were Jessica's daughter, I would still be at home snuggled in bed with your great-grandpa. But you are Adelaide's daughter. That changes things considerably. I saw the way you were fretting when everyone began talking about accompanying you. I knew you'd not put them in harm's way again, this time with Becky and Andrea in tow. Tonight was your only chance to skulk out of your house and into the library, and I planned on getting here early enough to head you off."

"I don't skulk."

"Yeah...you keep telling yourself that."

"I will have you know I drove over here, parked in the

back lot far away from any lights, and waited until I saw the last person leave the library. Then I carefully walked past the front doors, noticed Martha busy in the far corner, slipped in, Wicked in my arms, and avoided detection. No skulking necessary."

"Astounding since you are practically glowing in that outfit."

I looked down at my clothing choice and didn't think a pair of jeans and a grey sweater was all that radical—or colorful—that would cause someone to notice me. Then I looked at Adriana and realized she was back in what she liked to call 'my winter detecting and reconnaissance garb,' which she had picked up at the local Goodwill. Forget that she was in black from head-to-toe in a skintight outfit that would easily conceal her. However, the biker boots raised her a good two inches but were two sizes too big, so it gave her a rather clownish look. More importantly, her hat, bright green with a metallic orange pom-pom on top, would make her a beacon easily detected.

"Yeah, like that hat wouldn't turn heads."

Adriana squinted at me and pursed her lips. "Listen, missy, this hat acts like an invisibility cloak. No one pays any attention to a tiny person in a pom-pom hat. Anyone looking toward me would think I was a kid heading into the library and wouldn't bother looking twice."

"You do look like a kid...one that got in their older siblings closet and has clothes on that don't fit."

"Bah! You're wasting time. Let's get a move on! Andiamo!"

Adriana moved to enter the stall, but I cut her off before she could reach it.

I opened the door and went inside. Wicked followed me in and jumped onto the lid above the toilet. Closing the door, I assumed it would be exactly like the last time we went on this hike, and once I opened it again, I'd be in the hallway leading to Jerry, my fairy godfather, guardian of the Forbidden Library. I was confident in what I needed to do.

Squaring my shoulders, I opened the door. I found Adriana grinning at me.

"Hi."

I closed the door again and this time counted to five, then opened it.

"Me, again."

My eyebrows went down in a frown so deep it would assuredly make Bert of Sesame Street green with envy. I closed it again. I counted to ten this time.

"Peek-a-boo...I see you!"

"Argh!"

My frustration getting the better of me, I slammed the stall door so hard it came flying back and smacked me in the face.

"Ow!"

"Well, hello there. Need some help?" Adriana was cackling and wiggled her eyebrows at me.

"Why won't it work? I did this last time with Edith whining in my ear, and once I closed the door then opened it again, I was on the lower level."

"Perhaps it requires the brains of this operation to enter first."

"Then we'll never get," I smirked while my granny glowered at me, then she made a shoo motion to get me out of the stall. Sighing, I acquiesced and let her take my place. Wicked watched all this transpire with a look of abject boredom on her furry face.

"Watch and learn, Squirt."

Adriana closed the door, and I waited to the count of ten. "Did it work?"

There was no sound from the bathroom stall, which made me roll my eyes and exhale noisily. Great. Now the fiend would jog ahead of me, and I'd have to scramble to catch up. I pushed the door open and found a confused Adriana on the other side.

"Huh."

"Huh? Huh, what? It didn't work. Why didn't it work?"

"I don't know, smartass. This has never happened to me before. Hang on."

Adriana spent the next several minutes closing and opening the door with no success, and I could feel her agitation mounting. She spent so much time doing this, Wicked, becoming bored, curled up on the lid, and looked to be preparing to nap.

I only felt some moderate concern about the hygiene of doing this. Adriana gave the door one final try, slamming it shut and yanking it open so hard, she became unbalanced and toppled backward, so she landed hard on the toilet bowl —so hard her butt went a few inches into said bowl, and she managed to become wedged.

Wicked flew up and over the wall into the next stall, then skid into the wastebasket before swinging around and coming to a halt at my feet.

"Oh, *ew*. Great. I'm stuck. Help me out of here this instant. This is all your fault."

I gave my granny an incredulous look.

"My fault? You are the one venting your frustration out on a door. You can't blame me for being so doddering and aged you couldn't manage to remain upright."

"Says the dark witch who almost burned her house down, lighting a candle. Now get me out of here, pronto!"

"Listen, old lady. If you don't quit, I will flush you and consider it an act of mercy. They put down rabid animals, and you look like you are about to froth at the mouth."

"I'd like to see you try!"

"Don't tempt me."

Reaching down, I grabbed hold of Adriana's hands and pulled. She was stuck but good. I braced myself and gave another try, this time putting everything I had into it, and after a rather large 'Pop!' sound, out she came.

"Great. My ass is all wet. This won't do."

Stomping over to the hand dryer hanging on the wall, Adriana pushed the button, turning it on, then bent over and touched her toes, derriere in the air, in an attempt to dry the wet spot. And that's how Jerry found us when he pushed open the door and entered the restroom.

Startled, I screamed again, which caused Adriana to topple over in a somersault and land, legs askew, onto the bathroom floor. Wicked went into full Halloween cat mode and arched her back—fur puffed up in epic awesomeness.

"What on earth are the two of you up to in here? I could hear you all the way down in my bedroom! You were even louder than the television so that I couldn't hear Family Feud! No one makes me miss Steve Harvey's jokes...so you better have a good excuse!" Hands on his hips, Jerry stood in the doorway tapping his foot in anger.

I took note of the diminutive man and his ensemble of choice, which consisted of boxer shorts with tiny hearts on them under a see-through negligee and fuzzy high-heeled slippers on his feet. And I thought Adriana's outfit was outré.

Unfortunately, his negligee was so transparent, and I couldn't help but notice his boxer shorts didn't close all that well.

Great. Now I needed to gouge my eyes out on top of everything else.

"Jerry! Help me up. Why isn't the entry to your realm working?" Adriana held her hands out as Jerry pulled her upright, placing a steadying hand on her shoulder. He jerked his thumb toward me.

"Ever since this one made her daring jaunt to the

Forbidden Library, everything has been glitchy. Now have to use the service elevator."

The... what?!

Heads are going to roll.

* * *

"I can't believe it. I just *cannot* believe this... this... is total bull. You made me walk three miles. You made me walk all that way, sliced my hand open, spilled my blood for a pervy demon to taste so he'd open a magically sealed door that was supposed to be the only way in, and all I needed to do was take a flipping service elevator down to see Jerry?"

I was incensed at this news and fuming as I paced back and forth while the three of us, plus Wicked, waited for the elevator to return. The location? A locked bathroom stall that had an 'out of order' sign taped to it.

"Quit your whining, Liliana. I am just as surprised as you are. I had no idea there even was a service elevator." Adriana fussed at me while she kept flapping her hands, trying to dry her behind, which was still damp.

"Well, now you know," Jerry stated, "but you cannot let anyone in on the secret because I will be overrun by looky-loos wanting a peek at the forbidden stuff. It's bad enough the Sentinels are out of commission. If word gets out, who knows what will happen to me! One dwarf cannot keep the masses out alone. I will have to put a notice for backup with the Council. And as much as I miss the gossip I used to have when Edith was in charge, the last thing I want is to have to share my apartment with a stranger. I don't do roommates!" He complained dramatically.

Hold on a minute!

"The Sentinels are out of commission? What does that even mean?" I asked.

"When Mortimer moved in after rescuing that hot police detective—woof, woof—he must have shut them down with his vampire powers because they haven't been seen or heard from since... at least not to me anyway. Ask him what happened when you find him—if you find him."

While I was relieved I wouldn't have to face the Sentinels, I still chafed over the elevator shortcut into the lower level and that Jerry hadn't bothered to mention this last time we were here. I shoved a handful of jellybeans in my mouth and didn't offer to share them. I was so livid.

"Woman! Will you please stop waving your hands? Your undies won't dry out with your pants stuck to them. It's futile to keep doing that. Use magic already!" Jerry cried.

"Who said I'm wearing any underwear?"

I didn't need to hear that, yet somehow, I knew it. Those tights left nothing to the imagination.

Just then, the elevator dinged, and we piled in when the doors opened. There was only one button to push, and in less than a minute, we were down in Jerry's domain.

The doors opened to a foyer of sorts, but we could see through an archway to Jerry's apartment beyond. It was rather masculine, which surprised me considering Jerry batted for the same team—if you know what I mean—and was fond of florals, fuzzy pillows, and velvet furniture—that's how the place I'd met him the first time looked. The living and dining area was open concept to a rather fetching kitchen. Everything was sleek, industrial but with pops of color and kitsch, and I could not believe this was down here all along.

"This is lovely, Jerry. It's very urban chic." I stated.

"Yes, well... it's still a work in progress, but it's home. I am rather proud of it."

I looked around, wondering how we would go from

Jerry's apartment to his secret entry to the lower levels. He noticed me, and a crafty look crossed his face.

"You know, ladies, I really shouldn't allow you into the forbidden zone. Ever since Lily returned and the usual entry has become unstable, I haven't had to worry about anyone going in or something bad coming out. The Sentinels aren't the only things down there, you know!"

"Jerry...cut the crap. You know we need Mortimer's help. Just tell us how to get down there, and we'll be on our way and out of your hair." Adriana demanded, giving the dwarf a pointed look.

"Fine. But don't let anyone know about it. I managed to convince the Witch Council the Forbidden Library is temporarily out of commission until a meeting can be set where all the Elders can vote on what to do about an entry requirement. With Charles gone, I suspect they will be looking toward Lily, here, see if they will draw something up allowing her to vote on his behalf. Unless, well, Adelaide might be the one tapped for this task." He gave us a knowing look which made me realize Jerry suspected or found out Adelaide and Charlie's relationship status.

Adriana gave my fairy godfather a weighted look then sighed, sinking onto the chair in his comfortable living room. "Jerry, you always managed to out secrets and uncover things best kept quiet. I won't ask how you came to know this, probably when you babysat this one. But yes, perhaps Adelaide will be the one making that decision; if we can keep her awake long enough. Do you have any idea why she is still out of it?"

"I have thought on it, and I wonder if she is under a spell. I know she has been released from being merged with this lovely mini panther you have here," Jerry turned and gave Wicked a rub down, which had her arching her back in pleasure at his touch. "Perhaps her freedom from a furry prison set in motion another spell which is keeping her from fully being able to awaken. I can do some reading into such things, with the tomes in the Forbidden Library a scrambled mess. My small collection might be the only access to darker spells for the time being."

"Scrambled?" I asked.

"Indeed. Susanne has been organizing her end, and I've been spending most of my time trying to reset the rooms and pathways leading to them, gathering the books for safe-keeping when I come upon them. Still, ever since the reclosure and instability, the corridors keep shifting on their own, and I can't seem to find many of the rooms beyond. Thankfully you will find the central area accessible, and your Mortimer Snodgrass is residing there. Just don't ask me what form he's taken. He didn't bother informing me of his shifting choice."

After a few more minutes of chit-chat, Jerry led us to his coat closet and pressed a hidden button, allowing a panel to slide open. Beyond the doorway was a dimly lit hall that didn't seem to have an end in sight. I groaned inwardly and hoped this didn't mean another long walk ahead.

"Follow this hallway for about a minute, and it will lead to another door. When you reach it, use this key on the lock. Turn it clockwise until you hear a loud click. Then remove the key and place it on the little tray to your right. It will be whisked back to me magically and lock behind you. Once in the room beyond, you will see that you are in the room with the three archways. Take the far right one to the room with the cupboard. Mortimer should be around somewhere."

"How do we get back out when finished?" I asked, worried that we might have some strange or dangerous task to perform to ensure our freedom.

"On the right side of the cupboard is a red button. Push it, and a panel will open, leading you to a hallway that ends at this door to my right, here. Enter quickly, and make sure the door closes behind you. Go on ahead and open this door. I don't feel like having a creature or two sneaking in with you, nor do I want to hunt for you if the rooms decide to shift after you've been wandering through them. Try to convince Mortimer to leave while you're at it. I don't think he realizes how hazardous it is down there right now!"

Great. Just what we needed. A volatile grouping of magical rooms that might trap us at a moment's notice. My eyes tracked to Wicked, and an idea formed before we proceeded on our little journey.

"That's the plan, Jerry. In the meantime, would you do me a favor and keep Wicked here with you until we get back? I'm afraid she might slip away from us and get lost down there."

"Would puss, puss like to stay with her Uncle Jerry? Yes? Good girl. Of course, I will keep her here with me. I have some delightful cream and a tin of sardines that we can share as an evening snack."

Blech.

Wicked was already weaving around the little man's ankles and purring so loudly it caused me a moment of jealously knowing she'd yet to show me such affection. OK, so she bravely risked her life for me...but would a bit of love followed by loud purring be so difficult a task for her to impart?

"When you get back, just open the door and come on in here. The two of us will be snuggled on the sofa watching the Game Show Network."

After one last glance back at Jerry and Wicked, Adriana and I started down the dark hallway hoping for the best. It didn't take us long to reach our destination, and following the directions precisely as Jerry told us, we soon found ourselves standing before the cupboard.

Only something was very, very wrong.

CHAPTER 5

"It looks like someone tried to pry it open but couldn't. The damage is minimal, but the door isn't budging no matter what I try." I turned to Adriana to see if she had any ideas on what to do and found her glaring at me like I was an idiot of epic proportions.

"Move out of the way, Squirt."

I did as she commanded and just in time too. Adriana already had her hands up, and a bolt of magic flew across the small area and into the cabinet. The door made a grinding sound, but the hinges seemed to give up the fight as it swung outward, allowing us access.

"I hope there comes a day real soon where it's natural for me to remember to use magic. I keep forgetting I have it at my disposal."

I thought my great-grandmother would say something snarky as a retort, but instead, she gave my shoulder a sympathetic pat. "No one messed with the door. Look at this place. Everything has dents and dings. I bet it's from all the shirting the rooms are doing. Take out the Oculus Rod, and let's see what we find in here, shall we?"

Pulling the small wooden kaleidoscope out of my pocket, I moved in front of Adriana and used it to glance around the interior. The cupboard was more like an armoire that you could stand in with three shelves across the back. There were indeed the most unbelievable items on the shelves, and it would be difficult to name what they were supposed to be.

Mixed among the weird was the mundane—smooth stones, twigs piled high forming a pyramid, woven grass, and feathers. The oddities looked like twisted metal, crystals, tubes of an unknown material, with many that glowed. Some looked as if they were charred. Others appeared pristine. Nothing made any sense—that is until I held the rod up to my eye and peered through the lens.

"Grandmother! This is amazing! The minute I look into the rod, these items transform into objects I can easily name. Here, try it."

I held the rod out to Adriana, and she took a turn looking through it, peering at the items on the shelves.

"Interesting."

"What?" I asked nervously.

"I don't see a key anywhere, cara. Here, you try now. Do you see one?"

Taking the Oculus Rod in hand once more, I began systematically going from item to item and noting the changes to each. I went from the top shelf to the bottom but didn't see anything that looked like a key.

"Nope. Nothing. Now, what do we do?"

"I don't understand. Edith was under a Reveal All spell. She couldn't have lied about seeing a key, even if she wanted to." Adriana grumbled.

I chewed at my bottom lip and gazed at the Oculus Rod, as if it would suddenly begin speaking to us. Or point at the key. Of course, it didn't.

Hmm...key. Key. What else could be a key?

I began turning the kaleidoscope over and over in my hand and looking at the carvings a bit more closely. The palm trees, flowers, and the water...it seemed as if you were gazing out from a beach toward a bay. There were even two seagulls etched in the sky flying over the water. It reminded me of a tiny island that you could hold in your hand.

Wait a minute!

"Isn't another name for a small island a key? Like the Florida Keys?" I asked Adriana, who began to nod yes.

"Yes, they can be keys. You can spell them with a C, A, and Y. Cay or key...it means the same thing. A small island. Why?"

"Because maybe we weren't supposed to be looking for a traditional key for a lock...but something that meant or looked like a small island." I held out the Oculus Rod and pointed out the decorations adorning the piece. Turning back to the cupboard, I retook inventory. Sitting right smack in the center was a large pile of smooth rocks that I had barely made a note of before. Putting the kaleidoscope up to my eye, I cried out in amazement when the group of stones transformed into a tiny island complete with palm trees and flowers surrounding a central body of water.

Reaching for it, I carefully removed the island from the cupboard and held it up for Adriana and me to examine a bit more closely. As we stood looking down at the mini world in my hands, passing the Oculus Rod back and forth in our scrutiny, it did something incredible. The island came to life right before our eyes! The trees began to sway as if a gentle wind were blowing, and the water started to ripple and shimmer. Even more astounding was the sight of two diminutive seagulls flying lazily over the bay, just like on the Oculus Rod!

As I continued to gaze at the island, I jumped when a light in the depths of the water flashed as if something reflected the rays from some faraway sun. The overwhelming urge to touch the water came over me, and before I could stop myself, I reached out and dipped my fingers into the surface.

Carefully manipulating my fingers to pinch-grasp the item, I drew my fingers up and grinned in disbelief as a tiny gold key dangled from my fingertips.

"You did it, cara! Well done, my dear! Brava!"

"I can't believe it! It is a key! And it looks just the right size to fit in the silver box. I can't believe we found it." Tucking it into my jeans pocket, I wiped my hand down my leg and put the wee island back on the shelf.

"You did it, Liliana. Just as Charles hoped you would. At least, I think he meant for you to find it. I just hope we finally get some answers." I peered at Adriana and was dumb-founded to see her eyes mist over as she rapidly blinked to head off any tears that might dare fall. I wisely chose not to mention her moment of melancholy, thinking perhaps she'd feel embarrassed that I witnessed her show of weakness. I certainly didn't think anything less of her, that was for sure, but Ariana could be funny about such things. All I saw was a grandmother who profoundly missed her only grandson and the longing she suffered in the hopes of seeing him once again.

"Ok, enough of this... we're wasting time. Let's look around for Mortimer and get out of here before the rooms begin to shift on us."

Alrighty then.

"How do we find him if he's turned into a bucket or table or some such? Is there a spell we can use to reveal his glamor?"

"Not really. I'd just go around and knock on the walls or kick buckets, hoping one of the items we come across shrieks when we make contact. Of course, I could use magic to make silver ingots that we could chuck every so often and hope that gets the old boy up in a hurry!"

That seemed cruel and unusual, even for Granny. The last time we woke our friendly vampire, Adriana tossed one of Andrea's silver earrings through a gate and hit Mortimer right in the center of his forehead, burning the flesh away. It must have been horribly painful even though his body would regenerate. I would hate to think what a plethora of silver ingots would do to his person!

"No... let's not do that. We can try tapping items and shaking them and see if one of them is our vampire." I hurriedly replied.

Adriana smirked, and I knew she thought I was a big softy.

She wasn't wrong.

After fifteen minutes of going around the room and finding nothing that even remotely could be our hidden vamp, we had no choice but to move on to the next. This was the room that held the Ancient Tome on a pedestal. Only the book was no longer there. I assumed Jerry took it back to his apartment for safekeeping and was one of the reference books he'd just mentioned. As we continued into the next room, we began to hear a faint noise. Almost as if someone was groaning in pain.

"What is that?" I whispered, pulling up short and reaching out to grab onto Adriana's sleeve as she moved to continue into the next room.

"How should I know? It sounds like... hmm. You know, if I had to guess..." I didn't let my great-grandmother complete her thought because in that instant, the groaning became louder and more intense, and I worried it might be our vampire in distress, needing our help.

Rushing ahead in a panic, I left Adriana behind as she called out to me to hold up. Hold up? Why should I wait if Mortimer was in peril? Time would be of the essence if he were hurt!

Flying through the next room and continuing to the one beyond, I came to a screeching halt and found myself screaming yet again.

"Oh, my goodness! Holy batman...he's naked!" Whirling around as fast as my body allowed, I began to head back the way I came only to crash into Adriana, who went down in a heap of indignation and ire. I could hear the startled protestations coming from Mortimer behind me.

Adriana let out a loud, "Oof!"

It didn't help that I lost my balance and landed on top of her.

"Get off me, you big ninny! I'm suffocating! You're way heavier than me! I think you broke something."

"I am not that heavy... and if the wind got knocked out of you, why are you able to screech in my face?"

I backed off my prostrate granny and helped her to her feet just as Mortimer reached us, stuttering explanations on his condition.

I refused to look back in his direction and was well aware of what we had erroneously stumbled across. In reality, we discovered our dear vampire in the throes of ecstasy, with his paramour beneath him—another vampire, if I had to guess. She of the deep auburn hair, with nails and lips, to match. Her pale skin glowing in its unclothed state. At least that was the impression I got with such a brief look at the scene before my hurried retreat.

I was mortified.

Mortimer was mortified.

The only two who didn't seem the least bit phased were Adriana and the female vamp, who had snickered in a deep throaty way.

I risked a peek in Mortimer's direction and was relieved to see he had placed a blanket over his lover and covered

44

himself in a velvet smokers' jacket that made him look like an oversized Hugh Heffner.

"I am so, so sorry. I didn't... we couldn't have. Oh, this is so embarrassing!" I stumbled through my apology and wished I could instantly transport anywhere else but in this vampire boudoir. Where did they get that enormous round bed anyway?

"If you could give us a moment... perhaps wait in the next room there?" Mortimer all but begged us self-consciously.

"Yes! Of course!"

I grabbed Adriana by the wrist. Pulling her along with me into the room beyond, I kept going until we reached the one with the cupboard.

"Oh, my gosh, I definitely to gouge my eyes out now!" I moaned and sunk to my knees, palms over my face.

Adriana just cackled and patted me on the head.

"Get over it, kid. Even vampires get lonely."

"I will never be able to remove that image from my memory, like ever."

My great-grandmother continued her chuckling and pulled up a chair that I toppled over in our vampire-detecting attempts. She sat down and poked me.

"Get up and get yourself a chair to sit on. Don't make Morty even more uncomfortable than he already is. Better to just pretend we didn't realize what we just witnessed."

Yeah, right, lady. How the heck would I manage that? The sight of Mortimer's posterior would forever haunt my memory. Between his bottom, Adriana's revealing tights, and Jerry's boxer short malfunction, I was an utter wreck.

We heard Mortimer clearing his throat before he entered the room.

"I assume you ladies have something of importance to discuss to have come to these depths in search of me?" He asked.

"You got that right," Adriana informed the quivering vampire, "although it isn't every day you get to see the mating habits of immortals. I may have to write about the experience."

So much for Adriana having us pretend all was well and nothing untoward had happened.

Mortimer drew himself upright and looked as insulted as he could. He made a "tsk" sound and sniffed in disdain at my great-grandmother's witty banter.

"Very funny. I hate to put a damper on your jocularity, but your waggishness is not appreciated."

"Oh, get over yourself, Morty. We came here to find a key that my Charlie left hidden in that cupboard over there. We found it but also needed to find you. Despite your dire predictions about the prison conditions, we desperately need to get in there before the Witch Council blows the place to sky-high."

Mortimer looked alarmed at Adriana's pronouncement.

"Oh, my. This is not good."

"We know it's not the best circumstance, Mort...but I need to get at that renegade witch before someone eradicates her," Adriana explained.

Sighing, Mortimer pulled at his bottom lip and seemed deep in thought as he pondered what he'd heard. While we waited on his endless reverie, the female vampire made her entrance, thankfully clothed, without any indication she felt an ounce of shame. Crossing over to Adriana, she held out a long, graceful hand and declared, "I'm Caliente Saunders, charmed, I'm sure."

"Of course, you are," Adriana replied, mirth evident in her twinkling eyes.

Caliente acknowledged the humorous jab at her name then turned to me. "Ah! You must be the young witch Mortimer mentioned. You were the cause of quite the upheaval in these corridors; not that I'm complaining, mind you. I think some secrets should remain concealed from prying eyes. The magic the tomes contain is not for just any seeker to gain access. Although, if the power I feel emanating from you is any indication of your worth, perhaps it is to your credit that you should behold such spells."

Mortimer finally came out of his trance. Turning to Caliente and bestowing her with a tender look, he proceeded to reply to Adriana's demands.

"If you must enter the witch prison, I am afraid you will need a small army to defend you. At last count, your rogue witch had amassed at least one-hundred-seventy deplorable minions to do her bidding. Even with your power, Annie, I am afraid she would get the better of you. You see—if the number remained stagnant, I would not doubt the chance of your success. That isn't to be, however. That vile witch wasn't content to keep that set number of followers."

"What do you mean?" I asked with trepidation in my voice.

Turning to me, Mortimer gave me a melancholy smile.

"The witch ruling the underground prison has begun a breeding program. I have no idea how many abominable beings she has managed to create by now. They might number in the thousands."

Well, crud on a cracker. Who did Donna think she was? Saruman making Uruk-hai? This was not what I wanted to hear. And it looked like the Elders would get their chance to obliterate the hoards as they desired. There was no way our small band of merry magic-makers could take on so vast an army.

Right?

"Well, if Donna wanted a war, she's going to get her wish," Adriana asserted.

Right.

CHAPTER 6

"*A*driana has just declared war. I'm going to head upstairs and curl up next to my mother and sleep for a few months. Wake me when it's over, OK?"

I made this announcement to Lorcan and my Aunt Iona, who had been frantically looking for me, it seems. I guessed my espionage and reconnaissance mission did not go unnoticed after all. I entered my home via the front door and found them preparing to head out on a search and rescue but noted their relief upon seeing me. However, their concern came with something else; fear.

"Where were you? We have been looking everywhere for you!" Aunt Iona scolded as I paused in the entryway.

"Can't a gal go out for a walk around here? What's wrong?" Their frazzled nerves seemed a bit much.

"Lily! You did not just go out for a walk. I came downstairs to make Addy some tea. I pulled some of those rosehips off the little sweetbriar bush and brewed some. I spooned a bit into her mouth by teaspoon full, and she wants it, even in a twilight sleep! That was an improvement since I never managed to get regular tea in her! When I went to the kitchen and found the house empty, I checked this level, even your office, and while I was in there, I heard the front door open, so I headed back the way I came. When I entered the foyer, the door was still open, so I went upstairs expecting to find you in your room. But you were nowhere to be found!" Aunt Iona began wringing her hands and fighting to hold back tears.

Whoa! Something must be terribly wrong to have her this upset.

"What happened?"

"Addy. It's Adelaide. She's gone!" Iona cried and began to sob.

I looked at Lorcan, who nodded in the affirmative as I began to shake. He reached out to steady me but wrapped me up in a big hug instead.

"Your aunt called me. We've been looking all over the place for both of you with my parent's help. They are walking around the neighborhood. Now we need to figure out where your mother could have gone. We thought maybe she went off with you but then realized it couldn't be. She was only gone a few minutes. When she came back and went up to check on Adelaide, she found an empty bed. She had disappeared as well."

"You can imagine my horror, finding you both gone! And the dagger, too!" Aunt Iona cried out, pointing to the dining room table. Sure enough, the place where the dagger had lain was vacant. The other items forlornly sat as if waiting for the return of the dagger and rod to complete their group. That's when I realized the poppet was gone as well.

"But... I don't understand. Didn't you see anything suspicious when you crossed the yard, Lorcan? Was she kidnapped? How could Adelaide disappear so quickly?" I began to wander around the house looking under tables and in closets, hoping my mother would pop out and exclaim,

"Surprise!" Even Wicked didn't go off for a nap after spending hours away from her favorite resting spot. She went from the foyer to the kitchen, then back into the dining room, where she hopped onto the table and sniffed the area where the dagger had been.

Suddenly, she looked up and took off at a run. We rushed to follow her, all but sliding into the mudroom as she paused to jump to finagle the doorknob. She escaped into the darkness as we spilled out onto the side porch, but not before I flipped the switch turning on the floodlights.

There, standing in the amber glow, was Adelaide, dagger in one hand. And the other hand bled profusely from a gash across the palm. She held it out over the sweetbriar rose bush —blood dripping into the soil below.

I barely registered the sound of my Aunt Iona crashing down with a thud onto the floorboards behind me as she blacked out. Five seconds after she hit, Adelaide went down as well. I rushed to my mother with Lorcan on my heels. I guess we both figured Aunt Iona was fine up on the porch, but my mother was another story. I needed to heal that cut on her palm! But before I could reach her, Lorcan had already clasped his hand over the nasty gash, and a soft glow pulsed between the two. I didn't know he could heal as well!

Scooping Adelaide up off the ground, Lorcan rushed back up the steps and into the house while I checked on Aunt Iona, who was coming up out of her faint.

"She's OK... Lorcan healed her already. He brought her inside. Are you OK?"

"Oh, my! I didn't think I'd find her. I'm sorry I passed out. It's just, why is she still doing blood magic?"

Blood magic? Huh. I didn't even consider she'd need to continue doing that.

But I knew someone who did.

* * *

"I HOPE you put on some coffee. It's now way past my bedtime, and I can barely keep awake myself, and I've not been under a spell." Adriana proclaimed as she came into the kitchen.

"And here I thought you were preparing your war room."

"Nah, I've had one of those set up for years. So, Adelaide was awake, and now? Where is she?"

"I'm right here." Adelaide Croy Sweet stepped out of my half bath where she had been freshening up and walked into my kitchen, where she and Adriana came face to face after not seeing each other for over twenty years. You could say the atmosphere was sizzling with witch energy and over-powering emotions. They only paused a moment longer before they fell into an embrace.

"Addy. Well, well, well. Young lady, you have much to explain." Adriana had a severe look on her face that thawed to a misty smile when my mother stepped back then reached her hands out to grasp Adriana's. "I missed you so much, Trouble. What the hell happened all those years ago?"

Adelaide led my great grandmother over to the den, gave a squealing Iona a massive hug, then turned to me and shyly did the same. Then they all sat down—Adelaide next to her big sister, Iona, and Adriana across from them—I remained standing and slowly backed up into the kitchen to stand near Lorcan, my emotions chaotic. Wicked jumped down from her perch on the window seat in the sunroom and ran over to Adelaide, where she made herself comfortable on her lap.

Jealous? Me? Maybe.

And Trouble? Adriana's term of endearment for Adelaide was far better than my Squirt. That rankled as well.

I felt those old feelings of inadequacy mixed with uncer-tainty and awkwardness come over me again. Suddenly overcome with shyness, I wasn't quite sure if I belonged in this conversation and felt like an intruder in my own home—gulp—Adelaide's home! I knew this was ridiculous—but I couldn't help it. My mother must have felt my distress, for she paused and turned, searching the rooms until her eyes landed on my cowering figure near the refrigerator.

"Lily! Darling, come here. Come sit by us." Lorcan prodded me forward while whispering as I passed that he'd take his leave and see me the next day. Winking at everyone else, he pointed to the back door then left.

I nervously approached the three women and sat in the other club chair near Adriana. My hesitation and sudden onset of apprehension probably owed much to the fact that we would now have the answers to so many of the questions that had plagued this family.

I didn't know if I was ready to hear them.

"Addy. What happened? Freed from being bound to Wicked, you fell into an exhausted sleep. But it's been weeks, dear. Were you aware? Did you hear me read to you? Were you being held under by a spell? Do you know who did this to you? What happened all those years ago with Jessica and Charlie? Why didn't you tell us about Lily? That she is your daughter?" Aunt Iona lobbed one question after another like a machine gun, and Adelaide opened her eyes a bit wider with each one.

"Whoa! Slow down there, Iona. Give the woman a chance to catch her breath!" Adriana scolded and gave Adelaide the wonky eye as if to say; she's off her meds, that one!

"Please don't chastise Iona! I am sure you have an over-abundance of questions, and I promise I have many of the answers that must have tormented you all. Firstly, I want to impart just how sorry I am for everything the three of us caused. Before I tell you that tale, I need to understand all that has transpired in... did you say twenty-one years?

Forgive me, the ability to track time was difficult, joined with my partner in crime, here." Adelaide stroked Wicked, who continued to purr so loudly she sounded like a tiny motorboat.

Turning to me, my mother continued, "Then Lily... that makes you twenty-five?"

I nodded yes, and Adelaide's face fell. "So that would make me forty-two... almost forty-three come May."

"Oh, baby girl. My darling sweet little sister. You are still so young! I'm sorry you lost all those years to this horrible spell. Sweetheart, you know we live very long lives. You will have time to enjoy and experience wonderful things and see the world..." Aunt Iona trailed off as Adelaide's face crumbled, and she began to cry softly.

"Not without my Rosy, my Charles. I can't. I just can't."

My great-grandmother sat quietly during the conversations—she even appeared to be dozing off. But then I noticed her hand slowly point in Adelaide's direction, and she whispered, "Rivelare la verità."

A wisp of smoke trailed from her fingertips, encircled my mother, and then evaporated as quickly as it appeared. Adriana had a self-satisfied mien across her face, even as the other women stared at her in shock.

"Reveal the truth? What does that do?" I asked, worried that any more magic hurled at my mother might be one spell too many.

"I needed to make sure Addy was speaking the truth. I am not a Veritas. But I do have some truth spells at my disposal."

Turning to Adelaide, she continued, "I'm sorry, dear. But after everything that has transpired in both of our families, I had to be certain."

Wiping the tears from her cheek, Adelaide drew herself up, squaring her shoulders, and spat out a reply, "I would never lie. Not to you or anyone in this room. You should know that about me!" Her eyes flashed in anger and the air crackled with magic.

"Pulease, Trouble. Spare me the outrage. You are one of the best dark witches I have ever beheld. Why do you think I took you under my wing? Made you my apprentice? Unlike your daughter, here, you embraced dark magic like a magnet to metal. I couldn't pull you away from your lessons for anything. Well, except when you were out wilding in the wilderness with my son and your sister."

The indignation dwindled as Adelaide gave a rueful chuckle, "I was a brat. I'm sorry about that as well. You are correct. I dove into dark magic way earlier than most witchings had the right to do, dangerously so as you will find out once I've told my tale. And Jessica! Where is she? Did she not return with Lily?"

The room fell silent as we gazed at each other in astonishment. Did Adelaide not realize her sister had died? Wasn't she aware, while trapped inside Wicked, of the goings-on in Sweet Briar? Especially after my return and once I adopted my feline companion?

"Oh! Addy. No. We lost her. Our dear sister died last year of cancer. I never saw her alive again after she ran, after you all ran away." Iona's tears began again in earnest, and I jumped up to grab a tissue box from the half bath in the mudroom. When I returned, I found my mother had scooted closer to her sister, draping her arm around her shoulder to offer comfort. This dislodged Wicked from her lap, and as I handed my aunt a few tissues and took my seat once more, my persnickety cat surprised me by jumping up on mine.

Well, this was a first!

"I think it's time we hear the story," Adriana began, "but first, it seems you need to hear everything that has transpired while you were under that vile spell. It looks like I won't be heading home to sleep this night. Lily? Would you be so kind as to put me up here, my dear?"

"Of course! It is no trouble at all. Should I call Grandpa Antonio and let him know?"

"Oh, no. No need. When I received your phone call, I woke Keisha and informed her I might not return until tomorrow. She is on duty and will keep an eye on my Antonio. But perhaps you can fetch my bag from the car? Thanks, Squirt."

I begrudgingly shifted Wicked off my lap; so little time did I have to enjoy her rare show of affection. As I ran from the room, I could hear Adriana begin to bring Adelaide up to date with the incredible things that befell our family since the day she decided to 'run away.' Only, as we now knew, she never left Sweet Briar at all. This could take the rest of the night, and I made a note to get that pot of coffee brewing as my great-grandmother requested.

It was going to be a long one.

CHAPTER 7

"*I*'m still having a difficult time wrapping my head around all that you've told me," Adelaide said as she stroked Wicked, who was back on her lap. "Trust me when I tell you I know Donna and Deanna did all this...I can't say I am surprised by this news, only that we are related to them! That is so surreal. And Jessica...what a mess."

"I don't mean to pressure you, dear. But now that you know everything that has transpired tell us why. What were the three of you afraid of that you couldn't tell us? Why did you try to run away? Was it so horrible that you couldn't come to us?" Iona asked.

I glanced at the clock on my mantle and was surprised to see it was a little after midnight. We all seemed wide awake, however, and after refilling everyone's mug and fetching a throw for my great-grandmother, we settled into our seats to hear Adelaide's tale. Edith, my resident ghost, slipped in to listen, as did the spirit of my Great Aunt Moira, but they didn't make a peep.

"Before I answer all that and more, I ask that you hear my

story from start to finish with no interruptions. I will start in a place in this tale that will be unexpected to you and may start the question mill. So bear with me. I have a feeling my revelations will do more than shock you." Adelaide stared at the fire for the count of ten, then taking a deep breath and letting it out in a rush, she began.

"There was a little witchling who happened upon a book that seemed like an ordinary book... except this one spoke to her. I don't mean it whispered words difficult to understand before they faded into the wind, no. This book could converse, sounding like a woman with a rather fetching voice.

"It spoke of wonderous magic that was rare and hidden from the world; spells and potions that the young witch, Adelaide, could acquire if she'd only learn to read—and so she did. Shocking her parents with her learning ability and acumen in all she absorbed, they proudly told anyone who would listen just how bright and delightful their daughter was. This made Adelaide vain, yet the book whispered that she was right to feel this way.

"As the young Adelaide grew to be a teenager, the book pointed out sections where one could learn how to charm and beguile, bewitch and enchant...and the eager teen gobbled up all this knowledge and became proficient in these arts.

So much so that when presented to the Witch Council and her talents registered, they deemed her a dark witch of some repute. With skills too plentiful to list. Yet the most prominent seemed to be one so dark, they chose not to divulge this to her family.

"Adelaide, however, wanted to know everything they were saying about her, and as the book had shown her a spell to listen in on discussions, she was able to easily hear the

Elders while they huddled around a large table in their chamber. Because of this, Adelaide found out her strongest talent labeled her a danger to the people and village where she lived.

"The Elders proclaimed Adelaide a dark witch, and her unique talent was the Sirens Song."

Iona jumped at this news startling me, so I sloshed a bit of coffee out of my mug and onto my knee. Adriana looked shocked as well. Iona got so pale I worried for a moment she might faint. Adelaide, however, held her hands up to forestall any questions, and they settled—but not without some mumbling. Edith and Moira were listening in rapt attention.

"The Elders continued arguing about what they would do with this potentially dangerous dark witch, but in the end, and because her family was well-loved and eminent in their world, they decided to conceal Adelaide's most extraordinary ability. They chose to coax her, through lessons and structure, away from the extremes of her talents. The Elders, of course, saw it as a curse. Thankfully it was only a handful of Elders, those loyal to the family, who knew of her full potential and concealed it from the others in the Council.

"One day, Adelaide, who was a free spirit embracing everything to come her way, began to apprentice with another dark witch...Adriana Dolce. From another ancient family, this witch was mighty and one who could teach her how to control the darkness and temper the lure of losing oneself in it. Adelaide learned how she could be a force for good and seek out and destroy any and all evil that crossed her path—that she could become Karma in witch form. Yet Adelaide failed to tell Adriana much about the Sirens Song.

"It wasn't too long after this that a strange old woman appeared in search of a magical book she had lost. This old lady approached Adelaide, refusing to give her name, and asked if she knew of a book that could speak. Adelaide realized at once this woman must be a very old witch. She wanted to keep the tome away from the woman, but the older witch could read the truth in Adelaide's eyes even as she uttered, 'I know of no book such as this.'

"This only enraged the old witch who warned that because of this deceit, a curse would be placed upon the book, and if Adelaide continued to lie about its whereabouts, if she dared ever open it again to cast a spell, the curse would initiate."

Adriana sat up straight when she heard this, and I noticed she pulled the throw around her shoulders and shivered, even though the room was warm. Iona had her hand up against her throat, her mouth hanging open. Adelaide noticed none of this and kept going with her story.

"If only Adelaide chose to admit she possessed this book and handed it over to the old witch! Instead, she laughed and told the woman to move along and not look for trouble where it didn't exist, nor look for any talking books in her house. Adelaide's arrogance may have cost her everything.

"Weeks passed, and the teenager forgot her encounter, until one day, Adelaide needed to go visit a man who had been making eyes at her, following her, always. This man, Dillon Chase, acted like a suitor. However, he was already spoken for...he a newlywed with a child on the way. On this day, Adelaide chose to enchant herself with a reversal spell so the man would lose all interest. Reversal spells like this were highly guarded, but she sought answers in her talking book and asked it to give her a foolproof one.

"The minute Adelaide placed the book on her lap, opening it, the pages began to fly on their own, going faster and faster until the book cried out, "aha!"

It stopped on a page with a spell called Suitor's Lament. The young witch read through the magic and thought to herself, this will be easy, and I will be free from these unwanted advances!

"Carefully making the potion, Adelaide met her would-be suitor at his home on a day his new wife was away. She drank the potion, uttering the spell just as the book encouraged her to do. Suddenly, an urge overcame Adelaide to sing a song, and when the man opened the door, she rushed in and did just that. The older man was enchanted and scooped the girl up into a passionate embrace. Before she knew what happened, she found herself in his bed and the man's wife crying out in dismay at what she beheld upon entering her house. Looking down, she was ashamed to see she had not a stitch of clothing on!

"Adelaide cried and begged the man to let her leave—and he agreed. His wife's presence was like a cold bucket of water, and he ran out after the woman seeking forgiveness. The young witch ran home and told her best friends...her sister, Jessica, and a boy they grew up with named Charlie. This young man Adelaide truly loved, and he reciprocated. It was something they both felt since they were very young, which only grew as they aged. Charlie, dismayed when he heard her convey the horrible tale, wanted to confront Dillon. The young witch begged him not to go, so for a time; he kept his anger inside. Charlie had his reasons for being alarmed that his beloved was not aware. For you see, the same old witch who put a curse on the book had sought him out as well.

"Their paths had crossed many years earlier. Charlie, just a child at the time, had been tending roses in his grandfather's garden, and the old witch happened to be passing by and stopped to admire them. She asked the young boy if he'd give her one of the roses, but he was hesitant to do so because his grandfather jealously guarded them, and the young man thought perhaps he shouldn't give one to a stranger. The witch knew the lad's uncertainty had to do with the fact that these roses were highly magical, and she decided to use treachery.

"She informed Charlie that if she was given a rose, and he didn't tell anyone, his life would be well rewarded, and he'd have everything his heart desired. However, she stated that if he did not gift her a rose, he'd bring misfortune upon his family. Charlie had a streak of arrogance in him, for he was a very rare, dark male witch and didn't scare easily. So, he mocked the older woman, telling her to be on her way—but to take one of the wilted roses crushed on the ground and never darken their doorstep again. She was nothing but an old hag trying to cause trouble, after all.

"The old witch reached out instead and plucked the fresh rose from the young man's hand, pricking her finger on a thorn as she smelled it. Then she tossed it back in his face and warned him that if he ever married and had a child with a dark witch, one that could use the Sirens Song, the child was doomed to be cursed. She promised to find this infant once it was born to cast a spell that would turn darkness inward, so the child would become vile and do the evilest of deeds. Charlie scoffed at her words and turned away but paused when the same thorn happened to catch him and wedge itself into his thumb. Pulling it out, he turned to confront the old witch; only she was nowhere to be found. Tossing the rose to the ground, Charlie stormed into the house, sucking on his bleeding thumb, and put the old woman out of his mind.

He didn't see the witch creep back to take the rose he left behind.

"Years later, when his love grew into a passion for his beautiful dark witch, Charlie remembered the curse—yet decided not to mention anything to her. However, one day he was speaking with Jessica, sister to his beloved, and in the course of them joking, he mentioned the old hag and her dire predictions. Jessica cried out that she, too, had met this evil witch! What were the odds that all three of them would have her appear before them?

"The witch had found Jessica leaning up against a gnarled old tree reading a travel book. She informed Jessica that if she ever found a talking book or knew of where it was hidden, to take it and keep it safe until she could come for it. The old woman further stated she would know Jessica had discovered it and would reward her with a spell to make a long journey short and make traveling the world as simple as closing her eyes and wishing on the place she'd wanted to visit. In an instant, she would be there.

"The sister desperately wanted to be an adventurer and see the world...so she had promised the old witch that she would take the book if it ever crossed her path. The witch handed her a parchment that held a shrinking spell and instructed Jessica to use it on the book the minute she had it in her possession. When Charlie told his sweetheart, Adelaide, his tale, and they compared notes with Jessica, the elder sister was shocked to find out her younger sibling had the book in all along.

By that time, Adelaide had mastered all the dark spells and used the book with no further evil occurrences. She had even introduced it to Charlie, and they used to tell it riddles and limericks, which the book seemed to enjoy. Having never experienced another curse like Suitor's Lament, Adelaide assumed the evil spell was used up, and the old witch was all talk. But now, having heard both the tales from her beloved and her sister, she feared the curse was true.

"The elder sister professed she would never disclose that her sibling had the tome... but warned Adelaide to destroy it. Instead, Adelaide begged Jessica to take it and do it for her, for she didn't think she had the strength to harm the book, which had been her friend for so long.

Jessica did the one thing the old witch requested. She made it very, very small. So small that no one could read what was written in it. Jessica could feel in her bones dark magic afoot and believed the old witch could tell the book had been made small. Frightened by this, she ran to a small church on the outskirts of town and crept to the top of the basement steps and, closing her eyes, tossed the book down as far as she could throw it.

"The old witch never showed up. The three remained vigilant but uncertain of what to do next. Time went on. The three decided to run away because they didn't want any harm to befall their loved ones. The plan would be put into action when Adelaide graduated from high school, and they could make their escape, hoping they could find answers with a coven leader they heard about out west who was an expert at reversing evil curses. The elder sister had befriended another witch new to their town, named Donna, who told her of this coven leader. They would take the story of the book's curse out west to her and see what she could do.

"The young teen bided her time and went out among the village concealing the fact that she and Charlie were engaged. Instead, she pretended to be sweet on another young man, Chad Barwick, but told the poor lad, just before she ran away, to find himself a girl to fall in love with—her heart belonged to another. Chad refused to believe her words and insisted Charlie was evil and forced her to think the way she did by using his dark magic on her. So rare was a dark male witch that it was easy for others to assume he would use his powers to corrupt a naïve girl.

"Adelaide would not be swayed, and one night she left with her sister, Jessica, and Charlie and headed out west to seek this influential coven leader. They stayed away for months, and in that time, she and her young man went from sweethearts to lovers. When they met up with the western coven, the leader did indeed have the reversal for the curse but informed the couple that it was too late to cast. She had detected the presence of an innocent and told the young witch that she was with child.

"They begged the woman to save their baby, yet the only way she would agree was if they would never tell anyone about her. All three friends readily agreed, and the woman performed her magic, saying the child would be safe as long as the old hag never found out it was Adelaide and Charlie's.

"She instructed the young couple to marry, then placed an enchantment on the record to make it look like the elder sister, Jessica, was Charlie's spouse. She also told them to conceal the truth from family and friends until a time should come where the old witch had died. When the child came, no flags would arise since Jessica was not the dark witch, and the spell she cast on them would conceal the babe, making anyone who looked at the record believe she was Jessica and Charlie's child. Since the baby's powers wouldn't ignite until she reached puberty, she would remain undetectable.

"The three friends did all the coven leader suggested, and once the baby came, they presented her to the coven leader who requested they name the child Lilith."

I jerked at these words because I never knew my name was supposed to be Lilith, but I didn't interrupt my mother as she requested. Adelaide then continued.

"The three returned home and tried to live everyday lives, keeping the secret to themselves. For a few years, all seemed well until Jessica became aware of a horrendous deceit one day.

"The woman she had befriended, Donna, warned that the coven leader from out west contacted her, telling her the coven was coming for the child. The friend stated that this woman had decided she wanted the babe for herself, wanted to raise a daughter whose parents were both dark witches. And she expected them to give Lily up.

"Charlie, hearing the news, sought out Donna, but the person he found was Donna's sister, Deanna. She told him to seek out the old witch and kill her, then kill the coven leader so no one would be left who could harm his family. He refused her advice, fearing this would make matters worse. Charlie never liked nor trusted either sister.

"One day Charlie happened upon the old witch in the yard of his new house, and she told him she found him again because she put a curse on the rose that the young man refused to gift her when he was a boy. He'd taken a clipping from that bush and planted it in this very yard. The wicked witch had cursed the little bush and tied the young man's life to it from the blood remaining on the thorn from when Charlie pricked his finger. When she asked him if he had a child, he showed her the marriage record, and the old witch howled in frustration, for she was confident he would choose the younger sister as his wife, not being able to withstand her Sirens Song. He feigned ignorance and stated he loved only Jessica. The old witch left bitterly disappointed.

"With the old witch seemingly out of the way, the three wondered what to do about the coven leader. Instead of bringing this burden down on their respective families, they decided to take the advice of Donna and go into hiding— despite the young man's dislike of the woman and her sister. Charlie grudgingly came around and agreed that Jessica would take the child and run far away, disappear until she heard from him that it was safe to return. He would wait here and kill the coven leader. Meanwhile, Adelaide decided to confront the coven before her sister had to run, planning to eradicate the threat. She slipped away without the other two knowing what she had planned, hoping to use the dark magic she had acquired to smite this woman and her followers and save her little family. She left a note, telling them her plans and not to worry; she learned all she needed to know from the book.

"When Charlie found out his wife had run off, he ordered Jessica to flee, take his child, and await his call to say all was safe... never to return unless she heard from him and him alone. He would find Adelaide and help destroy the coven leader. When he departed, Jessica quickly packed, confiding the details to her confidant, Donna, and waited for the day of her departure. Donna was to secure some cash so they couldn't be tracked. Soon, Jessica left her home, never to return.

"The three had no idea how deeply they had been deceived. Jessica's 'friend,' Donna, turned out to be working with the coven leader—she and Deanna had been feeding the woman information all along. They also befriended the old witch who had restored powers to the evil duo that their own mother had suppressed, so not only were they grateful to her—they owed her. Yet they NEVER told the coven leader about the old hag nor the old hag about the coven leader. Better to have more cards on the table, they thought.

"Going back to when Adelaide chose to set out on her own, she was confronted by Deanna upon her flight from the village. A powerful conceal spell was slammed into before she could figure out her ally was anything but. Deanna was to give her a bus ticket for out west and remove any ability for Adelaide to be tracked. Instead, betrayal.

Accompanying Deanna was a man from the village that the young witch barely knew but always sought her affection. He was there to restrain Adelaide so she couldn't fight back. Before she fell under the curse, the horrid man wrenched a powerful ring given to her by Charlie from Adelaide's hand and put it in a little velvet box.

"He slipped it into his pocket, but not before she whispered a spell which traced through the air and wormed its way into the little box. Both the wretched man and Deanna grinned at Adelaide menacingly. Once the curse took effect, it bound her to a tiny black kitten that happened to be living behind the gas station on the way out of town. The evil Deanna told Adelaide she would forever be imprisoned in the cat.

"Deanna also offered to tell Adelaide the fate of her spouse. Charlie was to be auctioned off to a renegade witch coven out west and used as a bargaining chip to be the downfall of his family. Deanna would ensnare him upon leaving town. The only way he would survive was if someone would make a blood sacrifice yearly on the sweetbriar rose bush growing outside his home.

Without this yearly tribute, he would wither and die.

Adelaide begged the evil sister to spare her husband, but it fell on deaf ears. Just before she was bound to the kitten, the young witch uttered one last dark spell which allowed her to break free from her prison yearly, so she could give her blood to the sweetbriar rose, saving Charlie's life.

"Years passed, and Adelaide would awaken once a year to make her sacrifice. She did so faithfully without fail, until one day, the child she bore with her beloved Charlie came back to rescue her, break the curse, and allow her to separate from the kitten who had grown into a fine magical cat."

Adelaide paused and gazed at each of us with those last words, then surprised me by turning to look at Edith and Moira, who acknowledged her with a head nod. My mother, it seems, could see ghosts as well.

No one had dry eyes, not even my great-grandmother. Once again, I sent a silent thanks to my Aunt Jessica, who raised me as her own. Now I knew why she spent her entire life in hiding, afraid of shadows. Her sacrifice was incredible, and my gratitude to her was endless. I just hoped, wherever she was, that she was at peace.

Or even better, on the grand adventure she'd dreamed about before this horrible mess happened.

CHAPTER 8

"So, as far as you know, Charlie is still alive?" My Aunt Iona asked her baby sister this question while dabbing the tears from her eyes.

"Your guess is as good as mine. I don't think, in all the years I have been slicing my hand open, I missed one. I made the poppet with Charlie's hair and scraps of clothing that were his—even stuffing it with his socks. That little doll is the only thing keeping the rose bush healthy and Charlie from faltering with that wretched woman's curse."

"How did you manage to hide the items and write the spells we found?" I asked.

"Each year, when freed from being fused with Wicked, I had a full twenty-four hours of freedom. I used my time wisely. I knew if anyone saw me, I'd run the risk of the evil witch finding Lily. I promised Charlie to keep the secret. Just as Jess did. She left a note where she was heading and what her new number was, in a hiding spot in Charlie's desk, that only the three of us knew about. I called her a year later and told her what had happened to me and that I could roam free one day a year. I told Jess never to return unless Charlie came back home and reached out to her. I couldn't leave the house or yard. In human form, I was stuck here. However, I could go anywhere inside Wicked.

"We planned the notes and imbued the items I would hide in the hopes that Lily would one day be able to use them. I decided to leave the dagger—the one I used and hid in the desk with these items. Every year, upon my release, I would retrieve it and use it at the base of the rose bush. The other items I left for Lily to find someday. With my proficiency in dark magic, I discovered that the only one who could fully break the curse would be Lily. It's a blood curse—and only blood could break it." Turning to me, Adelaide frowned, but then her face cleared as she addressed me.

"I hoped you would find the ring, and I see you have. The last time I spoke to Jess, she told me she would send you here upon her death and hoped so much time had passed that no one would threaten you. It was a risk we had to take. With every year passing and no hope of Charlie's return, what else could we do? Harvey Rosen took that ring from me. Is he really dead? I'm so glad the spell I sent to it worked. You found me!"

"Yes, he's dead. I blasted him, and so did Adriana. He didn't know what hit him."

"I'm so sorry he tried to hurt you. I'm very grateful to Edith here. She must have been a dear friend."

"Um... she is, now."

"Please. Edith is Wilhelmina's granddaughter." Adriana stated, turning to Adelaide.

"Oh! Well... I'm sure there is a story there." Adelaide stammered, glancing at my ghost.

Edith rolled her eyes and began to pout. "How long are you going to hold that over my head?" She sniffed.

My great-grandmother began to cackle then tempered it with an apology of sorts. "Get your panties out of a bunch,

Spooky. You know I'm just messing with you. Edith has been very helpful as of late. We owe her much. Even if she is a pain in my behind."

Edith stuck her tongue out then disappeared.

I wrinkled my forehead in concentration, pondering everything I learned and coming up with so many questions. I decided to ask one now, but before I could, my Aunt Iona spoke up.

"I knew it. I knew when I saw the braided hair, some strands dark, and the other light red, that it was you and Charlie together, and not Jess. I recognized the shade of your hair which was always more vibrant than hers. Adriana rushed off with it to make a spell to call Charlie to us."

Adelaide turned to my great-grandmother in surprise. "And did it work? Have you used it yet?"

"Once...but not at full strength. But we were planning on doing so again—once you were awake and we knew what we were up against." Adriana informed her.

"You know...Hermione Winters asked me if I wanted to trace both parents when I took the strands of hair to her to make the potion." I informed everyone. "When she asked me if I wanted both colors in the mix, I shrugged off the red hair because I knew where my mother was at the time... or who I thought was my mother. We had just interred Aunt Jessica. So, I only had her make the potion with my father's hair. I wonder how far ahead we'd be had she used both. More importantly, what will happen if we use your hair now? I think it will be wicked strong!"

Adelaide reached out to pat my hand, giving me a warm smile. "What did you use to make this spell?" She asked.

"Well... along with the hair, I had to find a siren tear. That's what led me to Nichols Pond and the woman that lived at the bottom. She helped me once before, and she gave me her tears."

"You met Tarni?" Adelaide cried, surprising us all.

"You know her? Yes... I did. She helped me retrieve the ring. Harvey tossed the ring inside the little box into Nichols Pond. She helped me find it. Then when I needed the sirens tear and returned to her, Tarni obliged. She introduced herself the last time we met. She said her name was Tarni Vanderzee. Is she... I mean... you said the Elders described your talent as the Sirens Song. Is she really a siren? Does that mean you are as well... all of us Croys?"

Adelaide looked troubled, but then her face cleared. "There is a story there. Let's leave that for another time. It isn't mine to tell... it's Tarni's, and... others."

With that cryptic reply a pregnant pause in the room, I wisely chose to move on to another question, even though I could see that Aunt Iona wanted to continue on this vein. I caught her eye and gave a slight shake of my head—my mother was getting tired with us drilling her so. She looked exhausted.

"What about the magic to call my father? Why didn't he respond? I performed the spell and... oh. Heart's desire. Now I know why the koosh ball kept slamming into Wicked."

Wicked chose that moment to make a loud "Rwoor!" Breaking the tension and causing us all to chuckle.

"Yes. And that's when I figured out the rest of it...that it was you and Charlie, not he and Jess. Once I saw the spell go haywire and that koosh ball chasing Wicked, it all clicked." Stated Aunt Iona, "I knew. Right then, I knew. I just wished you confided in us, had faith that all of us combined could figure out how to deal with Donna and Deanna. And that evil witch and the coven leader! Oh, my head is dizzy!"

"Did Donna really kill Deanna?" Adelaide asked.

"She clobbered her, smashing her head to pulp, then disposed of her body. We haven't traced where it is yet. As I said, the skeleton under the porch here was a runaway—

another reason to confront Donna. I don't want Lily to be digging in her garden and unearth Deanna. She already has too many bodies racked up to her name already." Adriana sniffed.

Hey!

"Is my real name Lilith?" I asked solemnly.

"No, darling. We chose Lily and only pretended we would name you Lilith. The coven leader said Lilith was the name of an ancient sorceress from the Old Country and would imbue you with extra power. We decided enough was enough."

"Lilith was a name in one of my family lines a long, long time ago." Adriana snorted. "Not that I think they are one and the same."

"Who could the old witch be that wanted the book? Do you have any ideas?" I asked Adriana.

My great-grandmother pulled at her bottom lip then grimaced. "No. But I really would like to know and turn her into weeds on my front lawn. Then I'd let Antonio turn old Doc Warren back into a sheep so he could eat them up." My great-grandfather had a running feud going on with his old nemesis, and there might have been a time or two where the old devil turned the retired pharmacist into a sheep. Notice I did not say 'ram.' No one could prove it one way or the other, however.

"My goodness. I have so many faces to connect with the children they were when Deanna turned me. And others who I remembered who are now much older. I suppose you have called our parents?" Adelaide asked Iona, who nodded yes. "I suspect they will be here shortly then."

"They came to see you when you first arrived, but you were sleeping."

"I'm sorry I caused you all to worry. I could hear you fussing over me and felt the magic the Clerics were pouring into me. I heard you reading, Iona dear. I just could not awaken. Then tonight, it was like a switch went off, and I popped up, but in a trance-like state. It wasn't until I performed the blood ritual for Charlie that I fully came out of it." Adelaide fretted. "I think for the last few months, I have freely roamed more often than once yearly. But I don't know why."

Adelaide kept tracking her eyes to me, taking me in. "I can't believe you are my little girl all grown up."

"I believe I know how you are feeling," I smiled. "I think I understand the need for deception, but I am still not understanding why you couldn't disclose the truth to the family?" I asked her, offering a crooked grin to temper my words.

"Two dark witches approaching the Tribunal to enter a banns of marriage, especially at our age, especially having already eloped to Las Vegas... a human bonding. The news would have gone from one end of this nation to another and around the world. Lily, dear... I don't think you comprehend just how rare a dark male witch is. Charles is an oddity. We were afraid our families would caution us against the marriage... or worse, try to make us reconsider."

"But why? If you fell in love and wanted to get married and start a family... why would anyone stop you? Why did the Elders conceal your talent from your parents, my grandparents, and all the Croys and Muirs?"

I noticed the furtive looks being cast amongst the three women and became alarmed, although I managed to keep an outward appearance of calm.

"You know how you surprised everyone at the Council with your plethora of unique talents... many of which we have yet to see manifest in you?" Adriana began, "If they find out you are doubly a dark witch, our challenge will be to keep not only our enemies from wanting some of your powers bound—but quite possibly, many of our allies.

"Lily... your parents running off and eloping and coming back with you wasn't an issue when we thought it was Jessica. She was a moderate witch without an ounce of dark magic ability. Her talents were projection and clarity. She could project an image of a place once visited and help those who can transport get to their location safely. She didn't need that old hag's promise to give her that spell. She already had it in her. She also could free someone who had their magic blocked for one reason or the other, but that's about it. Wonderful talent but nothing special in a world filled with talented witches."

Adelaide reached her hands out and grasped mine. "You, however, are extraordinary. However, we are to blame—Charlie and me—for putting this burden on you. I would hate to think what the Council will do if they find out the truth."

"I'm not in any danger, am I?"

"Not with me around, Squirt. I'd like to see the Council try and stir up anything." Adriana avowed.

"It's not like it was years ago, anyway. At worst, I would think they would try to limit some of your natural talents by binding them. No?" Aunt Iona asked.

Adriana just shook her head and grumbled out something about enemies and upstart witches, then pat my shoulder and reaffirmed I was not to worry about anything. She'd be here to handle it if and when it came out.

Oh, *great*. Another thing to worry about.

"Two things confuse me. Age. Why was your age an issue? When you married my dad, you were what? Eighteen? That's legal age."

As you know, we are very long-lived, my dear," My Aunt Iona began, "Many witches wait until they are well into their thirties and some even their forties before they even consider settling down. There is rarely a divorce in our world because of how the magic is transferred via jewelry. Although the trend is starting to get younger and younger as more and more witches bond when they are mere children. As Addy did with Charlie, as you did with Lorcan. Oh, please don't deny it. I can see it plain as day, sweetheart."

I was sure my blush turned me an embarrassing shade of red.

"Lorcan certainly won't have to move far whenever you two decide to wed. He can just hop the fence and move right in." Adelaide laughed.

"Oh! But... hang on. When we rescue my dad, won't you want your home back, um...mother?" I stumbled upon my question. I was having difficulty calling Adelaide, mother, and the awkwardness was not lost on anyone. However, she chose to ignore my hesitation with grace. Allowing me time to get used to the idea.

"Darling... this is your home now. Charlie always planned on giving it to you. We would never have had more than one child. Can you imagine the mess at the Council if we made an army of dark witches? Don't borrow trouble. I think we will cross that bridge if and when we get him back." She ended in a whisper, doubt clouding her words.

"When. When we get him back. I'm not going to leave him out there in the hands of my wretched family." Adriana protested darkly. "But before we move on that... we need to get in and recapture the prison, destroy Donna's minion's and get her back where she belongs... in solitary. But not before we get some answers. I want to know who this hag was that caused this series of events. And who the coven leader is! I have some theories, but we need proof. And when I get my hands on them, I plan on squishing them like bugs."

You and me both, Granny.

"It also makes me wonder how much Olivia knows and if she has told me everything on her agenda. For now, we will continue the deception. Adelaide remains Liliana's aunt." My great-grandmother looked more troubled than I had ever seen her.

"Lily, you said you had two things on your mind. What else did you want to ask me?" Adelaide probed, releasing my hands and sitting back once again.

"Wicked. I don't understand how an ordinary cat could become magical. Was it because you were bound to her? And while magically combined, were you aware of things? How much could you see and hear and understand?"

And will she live a lot longer? Although that one I was afraid to voice, a twenty-one-year-old cat is almost unheard of.

Wicked had left our little group and was currently eating her food in the kitchen. Despite her continued aloofness toward me, I knew some of it was a ruse. After all, she did protect me from the Sentinels. In those rare instances when she would curl up with me in bed, my heart would melt. I could admit I loved that ornery cat.

"She is no ordinary cat, Lily. Wicked is your familiar, and they are very much like us—long-lived." Aunt Iona stated emphatically. "Why she is just a baby in magical feline years!"

I could feel the knot I'd been holding tight unfurl, those words offering me some relief. That was until Wicked decided to flip her bowl off the counter, knocking her food all over the floor.

"I guess my Familiar doesn't like her kibble. She doth protest too much, methinks."

CHAPTER 9

*T*he following day, I had an early start, much to my chagrin. I needed to mail a few of my art pieces out to my online customers. I had just landed a contract with a store down in the tourist village of Helen, Georgia. One of the shops there liked my wind chimes enough to carry a few, and the woman who ran the place called to inform me I had sold out, so another batch was heading her way.

Adelaide was up and had coffee going, which I was grateful for. She was off to spend the day with Aunt Iona, making the rounds and greeting friends and relatives alike. A tiring task, but one that needed to do. We hopefully could move on to some semblance of normalcy this way.

I did walk with her to the tiny Catholic cemetery where we'd interred my Aunt Jessica. Adelaide cried quietly and placed a beautiful bouquet on her grave. She wandered over to a corner plot that belonged to her one-time suitor, Chad Barwick, and I couldn't help but notice she left him a single flower. Now that I knew she never considered theirs a serious romance, I could look back on Chad's professing to me his displeasure with my dad with clarity. At the time, I didn't understand what he meant, but now I do.

Then Adelaide took her leave and met up with Iona while I headed to my studio, Found Things. The news of Adelaide's return had caused quite a bit more of a stir than it did mine, understandably. How often did one hear of a woman returning after twenty-one years having been magically trussed to a cat? Even in the witch world? Yeah, she was in high demand.

I had just passed my Uncle Stephen's café when I heard the door open and voices coming from behind me. When I glanced over my shoulder, I saw my cousin Nora with Wilhelmina Dietrich-Langsford and another woman. Groaning inwardly, I went to cross the street, but they stopped me before I could make my escape.

"Here, girl. What is this I hear about your aunt returning from places unknown?" Wilhelmina commanded.

Girl? Really?

"I'm sorry, may I help you?" I replied a tad haughtily or tried to, anyway.

"Don't be impudent. We are inquiring about your aunt. Surely you wouldn't be upset when we are only concerned at her welfare?"

I'm sure.

I turned to the unknown woman who had just spoken. She was wrapped from head to toe in some linen-type garment and even had a turban on her head. She looked like an old mummy, and I was almost positive I'd not seen her before.

"I don't believe we have met?"

The woman gave me a once over, then sneered, her disdain obvious.

"You did say she was rather clueless in a naïve way... perhaps she is slow or feebleminded, Willie."

The nerve! I felt my magic coiling up and had to take a deep breath to remain calm. The last thing I needed was to lose my cool and blast the group onto the next street. The funny thing was, while Wilhelmina and the stranger were rudely questioning me, Nora almost appeared embarrassed and ashamed at their behavior. Not overly so, but she wasn't up to her usual standard snark as far as I was concerned.

"Ms. Dietrich-Langsford, perhaps we should just leave. I don't believe Lily is interested in sharing that information." Nora uttered softly.

Yeah, see? Right there. That was almost polite coming from Nora. I didn't know if her animosity thawed a bit concerning me or she was off her game, but I suddenly had had enough of nasty people and their insulting behavior.

"I don't believe you are concerned one way or the other about my...uh... aunt's welfare. But you are correct in the fact that she is home. In good health, too, it seems. And we are looking into the circumstances around what happened to her. We have some interesting leads and will be contacting a few people that have information. I would worry if I were the ones who tried to harm her, in my opinion. My great-grandmother is in a foul mood and is looking to settle the score, as it were. I doubt we will be able to restrain her when she finds whoever did this."

There. Take *that*, you busybodies. I hope they spread the news around that we intended to get to the bottom of all these attacks on my family.

"Such rudeness. The audacity, and in one who had a hand in our Edith's demise." The strange woman responded. I moved closer to her as if I would get in her face and give her what for, but when she noticed my sweet briar charm dangling from my necklace, she reared back in a hurry and swished her hand as if she was dismissing me. I may have growled a little, and continued to advance but then paused when I heard a loud ringing sound like an alarm clock.

"Stop accusing Lily! This instant.!" Edith popped in, and I had to keep from laughing out loud. She took to heart my recommendation that she give me some warning before she'd manifest.

"Give it up, Edith. They can't see or hear you. More's the pity."

"Why! Don't you dare pretend you can speak to our dear Edith from the Great Beyond. I won't allow you to be so insolent!" Wilhelmina drew herself up in righteous anger and leveled a finger at me. "Young lady, you forget yourself. You think you are so special, but I believe you are weak in character and breeding."

"Oh, I don't think so. And thank you, Edith. I can handle this group. But I do welcome you trying." I smiled at the specter who was swirling around the trio with her teeth bared.

"Stop it! Stop this deceitful behavior. My granddaughter, was her spirit to return, would make herself known to her family. Not some failed experiment of a witch."

"Tell my grandmother I'm ashamed to be related to such a hateful group. No. They wouldn't believe you. Tell my grandmother, 'the lace doily was ugly, so I tried to dye it lavender.' That should make her take pause." Edith snarled.

I wasn't sure I should acquiesce to Edith's demands, but I figured I owed her one.

"Edith says, 'the lace doily was ugly' and something about dyeing it lavender. And she is standing right beside you. Perhaps only those worthy can see and hear spirits." I stated as I turned to leave.

"What? Wait. It can't be." Wilhelmina paled, eyes going wide as she sputtered in distress. "Is she really here?"

"Don't listen to this charlatan, Winnie. Of course, Edith isn't here!" The strange woman shouted.

I was going to ignore her question, but when Wilhelmina turned her eyes to me, I could not ignore the hope in her eyes. I might be a dark witch, but I refused to play their game and be cruel.

"She is. She is standing to your left."

Edith's grandmother turned as if expecting to see her granddaughter. I could feel the longing and sadness emanating from the woman and took pity on her.

"Is there anything else you'd like to tell her, Edith?"

"Just that I expect more from her than this pettiness. She always instilled in me how our family was ancient and noble, and I don't see anything of that in the way she and my great aunt are behaving. Tell her 'the laurel crown will grace the head of the victor, but only if they justly deserve it.' She will know what I mean by this statement."

I relayed what Edith told me and was shocked to see Wilhelmina Dietrich-Langsford wither and shrink in size and attitude, almost alarmingly so. I tracked my eyes to Nora, and she, too, felt concerned and placed her hand on Wilhelmina's arm for support.

"It must be so." She regarded me briefly, then seemed to bolster her insufferable attitude and brushed Nora's arm away. Banging her cane down, she pushed past me with her sister, as I now understood the strange woman to be, following behind. They didn't give me another look but commanded Nora to follow. With one final parting glance, the sister... Geraldine gave me a look with such evil venom; it had me wonder what the root of it was.

"Lily...I... Wilhelmina and Geraldine can be difficult. It's just... tell Edith I'm sorry."

"Forget it, Nora. I have nothing to say to you or for you. Not now, anyway. I'm sure Edith doesn't care."

Nora lifted her chin, but I could see the sadness in her eyes as she turned to follow the two nasty women. I couldn't give her any sympathy if she insisted on remaining friends with that family and ignored her own. After all, I witnessed the pain my Aunt Iona and Uncle Owen were going through. Nora made her bed.

What she didn't realize was that Stella Langsford Plank, Edith's mother, had dismissed Nora as not quite up to snuff for her family. So despite what Nora chose to believe, she is not so in their favor as she thinks. That was her problem, however.

I thought I wouldn't have any other incidents between here and my studio. Still, I was disabused of that notion when I heard a car coming up the street behind me and turned to find Deputy Gordon Delaney creeping up slowly, his window lowering. Ugh. Now what?

"You think you're so smart, don't you?" He snarled, glaring at me even though I couldn't see his eyes due to his mirrored sunglasses.

I considered ignoring him, thinking I'd rush over to Lorcan's mechanic shop, but instead, I steeled myself for whatever his beef with me was this time. I'm a dark witch, damn it. I wasn't going to show the brut that he had me rattled, not after facing the Sentinels and crazy Yolanda, among other things.

"Can I help you?"

"You can stay out of my business, that's what."

"I have no idea what you are talking about." Really. I wanted nothing to do with the man and never thought about him until he crossed my path. Getting into his business was the last thing I'd do.

"Give me a break. What did you say to Nora to have her break up with me? She goes off with you and that crazy bitch of a grandmother of yours, and next thing I know, she tells me we weren't meant to be."

"Well, I am sorry to inform you I had nothing to do with that. Nora was helping us with another matter entirely that has nothing to do with you."

"Witch stuff. How would y'all like it if I made sure the right people found out about your little operation up here. I wonder how quick it would take for them to descend upon this town and wipe you out? Ever think of that?"

"I think you'd find yourself in a lot of trouble if you think to go that route."

"Is that a threat?"

"No, it's a promise." I felt my magic coiling up again, but this time I didn't try to stop it from sparking and turning my eyes black. I could sense they'd darkened by the way the deputy suddenly jerked back in mild alarm.

"You think I'm going to cower from you, freaks? You have another thing coming."

"Can I help you, Delaney?" Lorcan was suddenly by my side. I hadn't even noticed him leave his shop and come up behind me. He looked like an enraged panther that someone poked with a big stick. He continued past me and snaked between two parked cars to walk up to the police cruiser. "I think the only one around here threatening anyone is you. Perhaps you should think twice about starting anything and take off. Now. While you still can."

"You know what happens to people who threaten the police?"

"Probably less trouble than any fool who would threaten a dark witch and the town and people she loves." He stated calmly.

"You people aren't above the law." He sneered then spit his tobacco out the window toward where Lorcan was standing.

"I am the law!" I proclaimed and allowed my magic to coil out in purple swirls, snapping and sparking as my agitation built up. I meant it too. For the first time, I realized what my standing meant. A dark witch fought the evil that came into their community and removed all threats so our people could live in peace. That extended to the humans who were innocents who lived among us that might get caught up in our magical world. This idiot threatening exposure and using his badge to do so put him on my shortlist, and high on it at that.

I glanced around and noted we had drawn quite a crowd of onlookers. June was standing outside her shop with husband Dennis and worker Maureen Kennedy watching. The snotty teenager was even snapping a few photos on her phone. Sheila and a few folks at the diner and at the pharmacy next door were milling around, giving us curious looks. Quite a few of the businesses on this side of the square had people watching and witnessing this minor incident. Many were glowering at the deputy. I guessed he hadn't made many friends in his short time in Sweet Briar.

We had quite the standoff going until I saw someone rush past me and over to the patrol car.

"Gordon. *Stop it.* This is getting ridiculous. Lily has nothing to do with why I broke up with you!" Nora shouted at the deputy, much to my surprise. I hadn't noticed her heading back in my direction, but when I turned to look behind me, her two elderly companions were on the sidewalk scowling at the commotion. Wilhelmina was, in any case. Geraldine looked amused, excited even... although she remained behind her sister and had even more garments on now, adding a wrap to her ensemble. Now Geraldine looked like a mummy in a cape. Her amusement turned to glee, especially when she saw Lorcan reach his hand out to snag Nora around her arm, drawing her away from the vehicle.

"Leave it, Nora. He isn't worth it." Lorcan stated firmly.

A look passed between the two, and I couldn't read them enough to see what he might be trying to get across to my cousin. Suddenly out of nowhere, a bolt of energy smacked into the police car, sending it over about two feet sideways and bouncing it up another foot or so before it settled back to the ground, smoking a little.

Deputy Delaney hopped out of the car like it was red hot or about to explode and rushed to the curb, all but leaping onto the sidewalk before he turned to survey the damage. There wasn't anything noticeable, except for the telltale bits of wispy smoke floating around his police vehicle.

"You! You just attacked an officer of the law! Dark witch or not, that is an act of domestic terrorism." Pulling out his handcuffs, he moved toward me, but my cousin Nora lashed out with a spell which had a chain of light fly across the distance between where she was standing near Lorcan and wrapped around the deputy's wrists, binding his hands together.

If that wasn't enough, Adelaide appeared out of nowhere and hit the deputy's handcuffs with a spell that turned them into dust.

"Keep your distance, officer. That's my...leave my kin alone." Hair down in a cascade of red, eyes flashing, Adelaide looked every bit the dark witch, and I noted her magic sparked the same bluish-purple as did mine. Her eyes, too, were inky black.

"You dare threaten our town and the good people who live here and expect us to sit back and do nothing about it? It's that harlot again!"

I turned to see the woman who had accompanied Nora and Wilhelmina pointing toward my mother. Geraldine looked disgusted. My eyes narrowed at her words.

We could hear the collective gasp from the bystanders,

but thankfully, Sheriff Buford came flying around the corner in his official vehicle, tires squealing in protest to reinstate some calm. Slamming the car door behind him, he took in the scene in one hurried glance then shook his head in obvious fury.

"Stand down, Adelaide. You too, Nora. Lorcan, you need to settle Lily. She is still turned. She needs to temper the magic and get control of herself."

I didn't know what was wrong with me. I could feel myself growing more and more agitated and felt my dark magic getting the better of me. Before I understood the sensations coursing through me, I felt this overwhelming urge to silence Gordon. He began a diatribe of slander the minute the sheriff was in his sites.

"Dangerous. All of them witches. How anyone in this town... anyone normal, that is, could feel safe knowing dark forces were controlling them is beyond me. I will make it my mission to let the world know of the secrets this town is concealing. Why I will...*gnawph!*"

Before anyone could stop me, I sent a spell slamming into Gordon Delaney that succeeded in silencing the deputy permanently. I wasn't exactly certain what spell I used on him, but more cries of alarm sounded when the witnesses took note of Gordon's face. Somehow, I managed to use magic that sewed his mouth shut. A sewing machine couldn't have made such perfect stitches.

Before anyone could do or saying another word, my great-grandmother showed up with Edith manifesting on her heels.

"Well, it's about time you let a bit of the wicked out, Squirt. And I couldn't have chosen a better target. Brava!"

I turned my gaze toward the two, and some detached part of me noted Adriana stopping short and uttering a soft, "whoa!"

That's when I raised my hands and called out the wrath from hell in the form of one intense storm. What went from a rather bland day, not too chilly for early March, turned into a tempest of epic proportions as the wind picked up and intensified into gale forces while the sky darkened and thunder rumbled. Lightning bolts crossed the sky as I focused all my attention on Gordon once again.

I didn't know what was happening and couldn't control myself. Some part of me felt horrified and knew I needed to regain control of my emotions. But another part of me felt alive. More than I had ever felt before, and my righteous anger was on boil point. Magic was spilling out of me, and I knew I was smiling as our eyes connected.

Gordon's had widened in fear.

I raised my arm and pointed my hand directly at his blanched face when suddenly I felt a light tap on my hip. Looking down, I recognized Tanaquil Alessi, my dark magic instructor, standing by my side with a pleasant grin on her face, looking around as if the world wasn't falling apart. The minute she distracted me, it was as if a light switch went off in my mind, and all my ire drained in an instant, leaving me a quivering mess and rocking slightly from having spent so much of myself.

"Hello, dear. Having a bad day?"

"I... I..."

"Yes, well, I can see something... or rather, someone has upset you, and we never did finish how to properly channel your anger so this type of incident wouldn't happen. Sheriff Burford, I take full responsibility for what resulted from my not properly training Lily. I will make sure to do so post-haste." Tanaquil, all four feet of her, was so calm but utterly in control of the situation, I didn't think anyone would challenge her. I was wrong.

"Oh, come now, Alessi. Don't pretend you didn't see what

happened here. Lily Sweet attacked an officer of the law. We all witnessed it. Don't blame it on poor training." Wilhelmina Dietrich spat out her disgust with the goings-on and wasn't going to let me get off that easy. "Sheriff Buford. Do your duty and arrest all of them. We need to call a meeting of the Elders to decide what is to be done with the lot."

"Oh, stuff it, Meenie. You always were such a blowhard." Adriana pushed through the crowd that had gathered and stood in front of her old nemesis.

"Don't try and turn this to your advantage. You don't want to get on my bad side, woman."

"You don't frighten me one bit. It's about time your family was taken down a few pegs. This little display of power just goes to show how allowing you to run roughshod over this town for so long has turned all of you into rene-gades. Now that the town harlot has returned from parts unknown, who knows what evil plans you've been cooking up. Many of the old families are sick and tired of being under your influence. They are looking for a new clan to lead them."

"Lead? Power? The only one speaking like a politician on a power trip is you, Meenie. Keep it up, and some might start to believe you orchestrated this little show to try and trick my great-granddaughter into doing something she'd regret. I was over at The Mystic Fox and saw the first attack come from your direction. Perhaps you'd like to explain that?"

Wilhelmina got a crafty look across her face when she noted the crowd seemed to be aligning with Adriana, so she backed down. His sister Geraldine, however, all but admitted it was she who sent the magic hurling in our direction. She gave Adriana the once over then sniffed.

"When did you get back, Geraldine? You haven't been around in ages." Adriana sneered at Wilhelmina's sister. Geraldine, however, ignored my great-grandmother and began staring intently at Adelaide, who returned her look with confusion.

Then Wilhelmina spoke up again.

"I don't know what you are talking about. We did no such thing. Come along, Nora. It looks like your taste in men is about as bad as your breeding. But there is hope for you yet should you continue to align yourself with my family."

With that, the two older women swept away up the street to their car, the driver waiting to open the door and let them in. Nora, confusion evident on her face, looked from me to Adriana and even over to Adelaide, then liked a whipped puppy, put her head down and whispered, "Yes, Ms. Dietrich-Langsford." Before following in their wake.

"I sure hope you had nothing to do with those Fredricks girls, Meanie. You too, Gerry! After tonight, you'll have some explaining to do!" Adriana gleefully shouted at their retreating backs. "See you at the Council, dears."

I saw Geraldine stiffen at Adriana's taunt, but the women continued into their waiting vehicle.

"Ok, folks," Sheriff Burford called out, "Show's over. Head on out of here. Nothing more to see."

Tanaquil had already released Deputy Delaney from whatever magic spell I enacted to seal his lips. The man had the good sense to get into his cruiser and head around the square and over to the police station. But not before throwing a look filled with venom in my direction. Another officer, who seemed to have appeared out of thin air, was going around taking statements, and I began to shiver as if I caught a chill.

"Lorcan," Adriana called out to my boyfriend, "Take Liliana home. We will meet you there shortly."

Not willing to fight since all the fire had drained out of me, I allowed Lorcan to lead me in the direction of my house.

Just then, a voice began to speak on my left.

"Never should get on the bad side of a dark witch. No good will come of it."

I jumped at the voice until I realized it was my handyman, Abner. Famous for appearing when I'd least expect it and tossing one-liners out like Captain Obvious at a rally for pointing out the palpable and clarity in any situation.

I began to laugh. Hard. Then my laughter turned into deep heartfelt sobs. They didn't last long since Lorcan placed his arm around me, and calm returned as his empath talent enveloped me.

It was time to head home.

CHAPTER 10

"*I* don't know what came over me. Argh. The people will toss me out of town. Or worse, I'll be incarcerated in the same unstable prison as Donna. We will run into each other in the corridors someday soon, and she will have her minions do away with me before I can say, 'boo!' I'm doomed." I lamented.

"Stop it, Lily. No one is going to do anything to you." Adelaide asserted and sat down next to me to offer support. "Not if I can help it. Do you think I will sit idly by if anyone dares lay a hand on you?"

I was shocked at both mine and my mother's lack of control and wondered not for the first time this evening if something was wrong with us. Dark witch or no, we both went into attack mode when calm heads should have reigned.

I was in my den, fraught with worry and missing Lorcan, who headed over to the police department to get some insight as to what Sheriff Buford's intentions were.

"Well, she has one thing right. She's going to prison." Adriana snickered.

"What?"

I shot up like a canon and stared at my great-grand-mother, who began to chuckle. All this did was make me suspicious of her words and ball my hands into fists.

"You suck. Do you know that old woman?"

Laughing outright now, Adriana waved off my anger like she was shooing away a gnat.

"You are going to prison because we are going to strike. Tonight. While the town and Elders are busy discussing your shenanigans earlier with me to distract them, you are going into the prison and will take care of the mess they, the Council I mean, let get out of hand by not admitting they had a problem in the first place."

"You have to come as well!"

"Well, I'm not."

I stared, wide-eyed in amazement.

"But you have to! You have more magic at your disposal than anyone I know!"

"Except your mother. And you." Adriana nodded smugly.

"Me? Me! I don't know what happened today! I don't have enough experience. How can I storm the prison and solve any of this? Donna and her thousand-monster army will probably blast me into a million pieces in five seconds flat!"

"Because you can. And you will. You will do just fine."

"You are insane! Totally off the charts. We need to start building a holding cell that can withstand this one before she gets any worse!" I turned to my mother, jerking my thumb in Adriana's direction. Adelaide was watching the sparring match Adriana, and I had going on with amusement.

"Darling. Your granny is right. She needs to stay here and head over to the Witch Council. She will be standing up for you, and me for that matter, and keeping the Elders distracted. It's the perfect opportunity to kick some Donna Fredricks butt."

"But... how?" I worried my forehead and felt my insides heave. I wasn't sure I could call up the kind of magic I let loose this afternoon again. "I thought no one knew where the entrance was?" I grumped.

"I have people loyal to me at the prison right now. Once there, my contact will escort you in—disguised, of course, as visitors to see an upper-level inmate. They haven't moved any of the prisoners out yet. You are still arguing the how's and why's and where's of it. Then you will get yourself lost on the way to the visitor's room and slip into the warded-off section heading down to the lower levels once you reach the stairs. Keep going down until you can't go anymore, and the blocked-off area will be apparent. Break the ward magically, and you're in. Just ask for Peter at the desk. He will know what to do."

"Hang on! How am I going to remember all of that? How do I attack? How many will be down there? You're just sending the two of us to take on what Mortimer called an army?"

Adriana rolled her eyes so hard she now knows what the back of her head looks like.

"Stealth will get you where you need to be to blast the army into a dust cloud. Surprise will be the element you need to eliminate them to reach Donna. She won't expect a small party. Heck, she is so sure of herself. She probably doesn't expect anyone to try to come at her. The woman is insane with visions of grandeur. Whoever is helping her must be planning some kind of elaborate escape. That's the only reason she hasn't made any move to fight her way to the surface. Haven't you wondered at that? She is content to wait. Which means she is expecting aid." Adriana explained.

"Wait! I thought we needed Mortimer. How did you find the prison?"

"I have my ways."

"Ways? Ways! And what is that supposed to mean? That sounds like a perfectly grand idea... not! How do you expect me to manage all this by myself?"

"The Elder in charge of its location informed me of its whereabouts. You won't be alone. You will have Mortimer with you. He's your secret weapon and knows the location of the door that leads to the lower level of the prison. He can also get you past the wards. Addy will be with you as well. And I am sending another secret weapon far worse than anything anyone could ever imagine." She sat back with a satisfied look on her devious face.

"My mother just woke up after being out of it for days! She's been in a cat, for heaven's sake. What if she's not ready? And what kind of secret weapon?" I was afraid to ask but did.

Adelaide placed her hand on my wrist and squeezed. "I'm perfectly capable, Lily."

"Adelaide will be fine. She is strong and competent, despite all she has dealt with. Isn't that right, dear?" My mother nodded, looking uncannily like Wicked when she's managed to outsmart every human in the room.

"Fine! What about this secret weapon, then? What is it?"

"Not what. Who. Antonio will be going with you."

I blinked, mouth hanging open.

Oh. Sure. There is no one I would rather have going into a massive witch battle, thousands of evil minions at the ready to take me out, then a stopped over centenarian gnome as a makeshift shield.

Somehow, I didn't like our odds.

* * *

"I DON'T LIKE OUR ODDS," I whispered as we approached what looked like an abandoned Dairy Queen on the outskirts of our town, heading due west toward Hiawassee, Georgia. We went north from the town square, then turned left and followed the highway about one mile. Then we turned down a nondescript gravel road and seemed to be heading back toward town.

As we pulled into a weed-infested parking lot, I peered at the buildings highlighted by our headlamps and was shocked to see it was, indeed, an old Dairy Queen. It didn't look like it had been in operation since the seventies, at least. Beyond that, I could make out the lights coming from some buildings through the trees. Mushrooms were growing everywhere, and wild burdock and daffodils were poking up out of the ground. Spring was well on its way.

"A Dairy Queen? A flipping Dairy Queen? What if some tourists happened along and saw lights and went in to investigate? How would the Witch Council explain a prison?"

"Shield." Mortimer intoned.

"What kind of shield?"

"It's rather like one of those gadgets humans use to kill bugs. Bug zappers, they are called, I believe. An obvious name if I ever heard of one. A light goes off and, poof!" he replied.

"Si... si. Poof!" went my great-grandfather Antonio.

"Poof? Poof! Oh my God. Do they kill the humans? How can anyone live with themselves around here knowing those innocent humans..."

"Calm down, young witch! They get zapped back into their vehicles with a suggestion that they need to head out back to town and forget ever seeing this building." Mortimer sniffed, looking disgruntled for having been saddled by my stupidity and nonstop worrying.

"Oh," I stated sheepishly. "Well... what are those building there behind the tree-line?"

"That's our town. We are directly behind the police station." Mortimer informed me.

"What? Do you mean to tell me all this time the prison was in an abandoned Dairy Queen behind the Sheriff station? How... what... why is it even back here?"

"Did anyone ever tell you that you ask way too many questions, young lady?" Mortimer mumbled.

"This was an old section of town that is prone to flooding. If you note the police station and the other building are up higher, and we seem to be down in a gully, and you will understand why they abandoned this part of town years ago." My mother explained. "Right over there is an old playground and a few more buildings that used to be part of the village—now hidden and crumbling away. All except for this one. I remember when the town voted on abandoning them rather than trying to get proper drainage back here."

How nice. Even Adelaide knew this mini ghost town was here. Why did no one come snooping around, especially teens?

"If a witch comes near these buildings, they become befuddled by a Confounded spell which sends them heading back to the town square," Mortimer said primly. It was almost as if he could read my mind. "I can read your mind."

Great.

"We have to park here and walk backward to the front sidewalk. There is too much rubble to get closer to the side-walk. Hang onto your great-grandfather, so he doesn't trip, and we will take our time until we reach the front door. The Confounded spell doesn't work if you walk backward."

This was going to be just lovely. I could already see an accident waiting to happen as my great-grandfather stepped out of the car and promptly lost his teeth onto the gravel at his feet. I reached down, disgusted about what I was doing, but no way would I let the old man try and retrieve them himself. He'd topple over and get injured! Handing the now gritty teeth over, I was repulsed to see

97

him spit on the shiny white snappers and pop them back into his mouth. He gave me a wide grin, and his teeth fell out once more.

"Oopa!"

This was going to be a long night.

We managed to walk carefully backward without once glancing over our shoulders and all but stumbled to a door that looked like it hadn't opened since nineteen-seventy-four. The sign on the door was lopsided and stated the business was closed. No kidding. Nixon was in office the last time this place served food, I'm sure.

I noticed my great-grandfather had moved back a bit, searched the parking lot, and then looked up to the sky. The minute he turned back toward us, he popped out of existence and wound up in the backseat of Mortimer's hearse.

Yes. Mortimer drove. A hearse. Try looking inconspicuous wandering through town in a massive black hearse with a vampire at the wheel. I'm still amazed no one spotted us.

"I'll go get him." Mortimer sighed.

Going back the way he had come, Mortimer reached his vehicle and opened the door for Antonio, who just smiled at him and blinked. Gently guiding my great-grandfather backward, it took the vampire about two solid minutes to reach us again.

"Ok. Now that we have that bit of fun over with, I suggest we go over the plan of action once more before we enter. Visiting hours are over in one hour. Let's..." Mortimer trailed off as it registered to us once more that Antonio was no longer among us. Indeed, we could just see his head poking up above the headrest in the backseat of the hearse once more.

"Why does he keep walking back toward the curb then turning around. Doesn't he understand the minute he does, he goes poof? Didn't he agree to no poofing?" I gritted the words out through my teeth.

"A moment." Mortimer loped back to his car and once again carefully led Antonio back to where we were standing, then slowly turned him around so he was facing us.

"Buona Notte!" Antonio acted like he hadn't seen us in quite some time, and I wondered at the mental state of Adriana for calling this our' secret weapon.' Especially seeing as how his teeth were nowhere to be found. He was all gums. Happy, at least. But still.

"Where are his bloody *teeth*?" I whispered furiously.

"Probably back in the car. But no matter. He doesn't need teeth to help us eradicate a few thousand bad guys." Mortimer groused.

Adelaide just chuckled.

I held onto Antonio, preventing him from trotting back to the curb while Mortimer went over a few plans of attack.

"Liliana. Vieni qua. Coma here." Pointing up to the sky, my great-grandfather had me gazing at the moon, full and bright in the night sky. "Guarda la bella luna, Liliana. You look."

I looked alright and wondered why he asked me to.

"You see? La luna ha bisogno di mostrarci qualcosa! You look where it shines, no?" Antonio peered at Mortimer, who seemed to understand what my great-grandfather was trying to tell us. Turning back towards the parked car, Mortimer stood in silence a full minute, then sighed. Backing up to the building, he slowly turned and addressed us.

"Oh my. This is not good. Adelaide, do me a favor and shine a light on that tree near where we parked so you can see what I'm looking at." Mortimer commanded.

My mother cast a spell, and a softly glowing orb appeared in the sky. It floated over to the tree about twenty feet from where we parked. As the orb drew closer to the tree, I thought I saw what looked like a scarecrow dangling on a nearby branch. Then I felt the color draining from my face.

"You think so, Morty? This spells disaster. No pun intended."

There, hanging from a tree branch and not at all a scarecrow, but a body with a noose tight around his neck, was one very dead Deputy Gordon Delaney.

Somehow, I didn't think we'd be heading into the prison tonight. Call it an educated guess, if you will.

"Wait. Where's... oh."

Antonio was peeking over the back seat and waving at us, holding up his lost dentures once again.

At least one of us was oblivious. I was kind of jealous of the old witch.

CHAPTER 11

"*E*xplain to me again just what the four of you were doing out behind the police station at eight o'clock in the evening?" Sheriff Buford did not seem remotely amused at finding the four of us at a crime scene, one of his deputies the victim, and two of the people that called it in happened to be two of the three who'd confronted the man earlier in the day.

Yeah, even I was suspicious.

"Would you believe me if I told you they were giving me dark witch lessons?" I asked.

Sheriff Buford squinched his face into a confused look and scratched his head with his hat in hand.

"Lily. I don't know what you are up to, but this doesn't look good."

Oh, do you think so?

"Sheriff, you can't possibly believe the four of us would come out here, kill Gordon, then call it in. Why would we be that stupid?"

"After today's little performance? What am I supposed to

think? Oh, I don't know what to do about this. Why couldn't y'all just stay at your place and out of my hair?" Seeing as how he was going bald on top. Yeah, I was catty in moments of stress. Sue me.

Eying Mortimer, he continued, "Gordon is... was... a big guy. It would take someone with extra strength to get him up in that tree."

"Magic could get him up in that tree, Sheriff," Adelaide stated and stepped in front of Mortimer to make Glen take notice of her and remove his gaze from our vampire friend. I noticed Glen blush and remembered he was one of the many men in town bewitched by my mother. He gulped loudly, then sighed once more.

Walking over to the body, Sheriff Buford began searching the ground and peered up at the gruesome sight a few times. He got up close and personal, closer than I would ever be comfortable with, and did a preliminary examination of the body. Then he came back over to the four of us huddling near the hearse.

"And in that car, too. What were you thinking?" Glen shook his head. You four are lucky sons of bi... um, you are fortunate I happened to look out the front of the police department and spied this vehicle with that one at the wheel heading out of town. You are also lucky it doesn't have tinted windows because I saw you in the front, Lily, and Adelaide's red hair in the back seat. I am going to assume Antonio was in there with you since he should probably be in a booster seat." He paused, shaking his head once more, then slapped his hat against his knee before continuing.

"There was no way you could have killed Gordon. Rigor Mortis has set in, which means he's been out here at least six to eight hours. He stormed out of my office not too soon after I got back in. That means he must have died... er, rather, was killed right after he left. You were at your home because I made sure Lorcan got you there safe and sound. And I noted Adelaide was with you as well as Adriana. I put a deputy on your house to make sure none of them Langsford's or Planks showed up. That clears most of your gang. Lorcan has been with me all this time, although I am hesitant to tell him what I found on this call. He's climbing the walls wondering, I'm sure."

I gulped at hearing this because I forgot to text him, letting him in on Adriana's plans for me this evening in all the hoopla. He was not going to be pleased.

"So... we can leave?" I tentatively asked.

"Not until you four tell me what you were doing out here in this abandoned lot."

I started, tracking my eyes over to Adelaide, who seemed equally surprised the sheriff seemed not to know we were standing a hundred yards away from the entrance to the witch prison. He either didn't know or was waiting to see what we would say before admitting to anything.

"Sheriff. We really are showing Lily how to harness and control her dark magic better. Adriana thought it best to keep her away from where an errant spell could harm an innocent." Adelaide explained, pointing to herself, Mortimer and Antonio.

"What the heck are you supposed to be, anyway? You look like Lurch or that dude in the James Bond movies with all those teeth." Sheriff Buford asked.

"Jaws," I mumbled.

"What's that?"

"Jaws. The man in the James Bond movie's character was called Jaws. He had metal teeth." I explained.

The sheriff just squinted at me some more, then he sighed so long it turned into a groan.

"I don't have time for movie trivia. I need to explain this somehow without your names being involved. You. Big guy. I saw you at the search and rescue for Brian Chase, so I assume you are tight with this lot. I need you to take the heat for them and be the one who called this in."

"I am the one who called this in," Mortimer replied in a gravelly voice.

The sheriff reared back, seemingly shocked that Mortimer could speak at all.

"Oh! Well... yes. Good, good. So, you called this in because you were out here... what?"

"Communing with the night creatures, perhaps?" Mortimer offered.

"You are a night creature," I whispered in sotto voice.

"Wait. Don't tell me he's a vampire. Oh, lovely. Do you know how this town is going to react if news of this gets out? I can't just let you all go because the call came in, and someone has to be that person."

We stood there a minute deep in contemplation when Antonio decided to speak up.

"I call—you no make-a the call. I make-a the call. Capisci?" He took Mortimer's phone, making sure his prints were all over it, then handed it to Sheriff Burford. "You let they go home now, and I go with to La Stazione di Polizia. Ok? Ok!"

Huh. That was the best idea I heard all day.

* * *

"What do you mean you left him with the sheriff? How could you leave my husband behind and make him take the wrap? I can't believe this!" Adriana was frothing at the mouth, and in utter amazement, we abandoned Antonio to his fate.

"Adriana. This was the best we could come up with. He

came up with it, actually. Mortimer would be staked and buried alive. I would have been arrested, Lily too, at least until Sheriff Glen could calm everyone down and explain how we happened upon the body. This way, it keeps us out of it, and Antonio... well, no one would dream such a tiny man would be able to handle the body. Gordon was already dead when he was placed in that tree. That's what Glen said, anyway." Adelaide explained.

"Antonio has already been cleared because the sheriff explained in the official report that he called him up asking him to gather some mushrooms since Antonio is an expert. This way, no one will suspect any wrongdoing, and it explains why he was out there and discovered the body. It was very fast-thinking on Glen's part, if I may say so." She finished and smiled at Adriana.

My great-grandmother still wasn't satisfied, worrying that Antonio might still be targeted as a murderer even though the sheriff came up with a pretty good alibi.

"How do we explain the cell phone? It is going in the records as belonging to a Mortimer Snodgrass. Why would Antonio have it?" she asked.

"Because I gave it to him in case he became turned around?" Mortimer offered. "After all, he gave me my first one, so it is only decent that I lend him mine."

"The Elders are going to have a field day with this. I just know it. You are all lucky Keisha swooped in and got Antonio out of there." Adriana complained.

"I think Nora did it," Andrea stated darkly. She arrived right as we returned home, having gone a roundabout way to not be anywhere in the vicinity of the town square or police department. Lorcan was here as well, and I was correct in assuming he'd be pissed. He was tight-lipped and scowling at everyone. Antonio was already home and in bed. Adriana had called Keisha to come to retrieve the older man and get him safely back to their Victorian on the other side of town.

"How did the meeting go?"

"How do you think?" Adriana spat out. "Stella Langsford was there, going on and on about the 'unstable Dolce clan which includes a few Croys as well.' She asked that an investigation be opened and our dark magic abilities bound until further notice. Thankfully not many in attendance paid her much attention. But a few? I can almost hand pick the families that are siding with Wilhelmina and her coup attempt." Adriana was now pacing back and forth. Wicked was on the mantle, following her every move.

"More importantly, it had to be Wilhelmina behind this. I think she murdered Gordon to set the lot of you up. The timing and placement are too perfect."

"What do you mean?" I asked.

"This morning, when I confronted Wilhelmina, I all but told her we planned on hitting the prison to find Donna. She understood the meaning behind my words. She took advantage of this knowledge and tried to set one of us up for murder!"

A chilling thought.

Could it be true? I knew she hated Adriana and would stop at nothing to have her family move up to the top position in this town. But murder? And what about Nora? Was Andrea correct, and Nora had a part in it? After all, she was Gordon's ex, and they always say to look at those closest to the victim. I just couldn't see it, though, despite our differences. I didn't think Nora would resort to murder. Plus, she almost seemed contrite today. Like she wanted to mend some fences, perhaps.

Edith, who was hovering near the fireplace, came drifting over to me and whispered in my ear. "I'm going to go spy on my family. Who better than I to find out what they are up to?

Maybe I can get insight into what happened and if one of them is guilty."

My helpful ghost popped out of the room with those words, leaving me troubled and wondering what the next day would bring.

CHAPTER 12

The following day, I awoke to a text message coming across my cell phone. It was Adriana, and she wanted me to hurry up and meet her at Joe's Diner for breakfast. Groaning, I sat up and was surprised not to find Wicked anywhere on my bed. I hurried into the bathroom and showered, pulling my still-damp hair into a ponytail. Tossing on a sweater and jeans, I ran downstairs, calling out to my errant cat.

Nothing.

"Fine! I'm leaving you kibble in your bowl, and there is fresh water."

Rushing to my new Jeep, I paused and took her in with the morning sun making her burnt metallic orange paint job glow and sparkle. I loved my new purchase even though it was an extravagance. I still squirmed thinking about how I had come to purchase said Jeep... but that was a long story best left for another time.

Hopping in, I drove the short distance to the diner, waving at Gordy Polk as he made his rounds collecting trash and parked on the square, across the street from it. Looking both ways, I was just about to step off the curb when I looked up and saw June Carter waving at me from inside the restaurant. I waved back and smiled, indicating I was heading in.

Sheila Polk handed me a menu the minute I came through the door and pointed to Adriana sitting with my mother and June across from them. In my rush to leave the house, I totally forgot about my mother and felt a moment's guilt; I checked on the cat but didn't look in on Adelaide! Speaking of said cat, sitting in between my mother and great-grandmother was Wicked, looking superior and smug at the same time.

"Do I even want to know how she got here?" I asked the group, glowering at the cat while everyone else gave her a fond look. All but Adriana. She looked like she'd been chewing nails and spitting them out. "Isn't this against some kind of health code?"

"Only if someone complains, and no one would dare. Wicked is a heroine...saving us and facing off against those nasty Sentinels!" Adelaide purred while Wicked ate it up.

Sitting quietly in my spot, I couldn't help overhearing several conversations at nearby tables. All that anyone seemed to be talking about was the murder of Deputy Delaney. It didn't go unnoticed by me that more than a few eyes peered in my direction then hurriedly looked away when I met their glance. Notoriety strikes again.

"I don't know why folks in this town think we always have something to do with every murder." I grumped.

"Maybe because many connect to us in one way or the other," Adriana noted.

"We had nothing to do with Gordon's demise!"

"Not directly, but again...was it a set-up against this family? Was it a warning of some kind? If so, connected to us."

"And you did attack him in public...and with magic. Not that I blame you!" June commiserated.

"Well, this sucks." I pouted.

"Yeah, well, tell that to Gordon." Adriana laughed. "You let out your wicked to play, cara. The town reeled seeing such a powerful display. But they know of your worth now. You will get some stares and awkward moments, but you'll be fine. People get used to it."

"Well... that's not going to make me feel any better... and I am not mourning that man!"

Look, I was sorry someone murdered Gordon. But I wasn't going to get weepy over the fact someone killed him. No one deserved that, but I was no hypocrite. The man was horrid to me. It was rather difficult for me to bring up much sympathy.

"Ladies. Good morning."

Looking up, I was surprised to see Brian Chase. With him was a middle-aged man with a kindly smile sporting plenty of laugh lines.

"Brian! How do you feel? Are you all healed?" June inquired.

As mentioned, Brian had been in the horrific predicament of being dropped into an abyss where his body would wither, and he would slowly and tragically end, his soul left behind in a wraith-like existence. If it weren't for Mortimer, we would have lost him. It took several days to get him to awaken, not unlike my mother, but he seemed well standing here looking all healthy... and hot. Hey! I couldn't change that reality.

"I'm getting there. I am on this latest case. Sheriff Buford is beside himself with this one. How one of his men could wind up dead and hanged behind the police station." Turning to the man beside him, he introduced us.

"This is Doctor Clarkston. Our new medical examiner...another one of us." Brian added, lowering his voice a tad. "We will be working on this case until it's solved."

"Would you care to join us?" Adelaide asked.

Adriana frowned but didn't say a word.

Brian paused, not answering for a bit longer than seemed polite, but then he agreed, apologizing for his behavior. "Please forgive me. I am just amazed to see you alive and well again. I remember you, even though I was seven when you disappeared, and, quite frankly, you almost look precisely the same."

Adelaide laughed in delight, full flirt mode on, which made me see what the men of this town were up against when she turned her eyes their way.

"Aren't you sweet? I remember you as well. Brian...so much do you resemble your father. I am sorry." Adelaide reached out, placing her hand over Brian's and offering quiet sympathy and nothing else. After all, it was a tense topic and one I'd rather not focus on for now.

"Thank you."

Addressing the rest of us, Brian lowered his voice even more so that we all had to lean in to hear his following words. "I don't want this getting out to the community, but there are...er...some irregularities with Deputy Delaney's case, and I need to gather the family together to discuss it...in private." Tracking his eyes around the diner, he, too, noticed most of the patrons had quieted down, hoping to hear a tidbit or two from us. The gossip mill is going into full active mode, it seems.

Doctor Clarkston had been sipping the coffee Sheila brought over to him when he suddenly noticed Wicked sitting across from him. "That's a cat." He stated rather obviously.

"No shi..."

"Granny!" I loudly cut off her next words.

"Pardon." The good doctor explained. "What I meant is, this cat is a familiar and a strong one too. You see... one of my talents is identifying familiars over everyday pets. Sometimes in this business, and our world, if I come upon a deceased soul and they had pets, the Council uses me to separate a familiar from a normal family pet. This way, we can care for the familiar, moving them to a safe facility."

"I don't understand. What does this mean? Please tell me you don't just leave the regular animals behind to fend for themselves. What kind of facility?" I worried, giving the doctor my full attention.

He became confused, then his face cleared. "Ah... you must be the young lady I've heard just came back to the fold. Didn't grow up a witch, did you? Well, no worries. It's not what you think. The family of a witch who has passed on sometimes hasn't been in the household with their loved one and doesn't know which pets are familiars. All of the animals are cared for. Several families take the normal pets. But a familiar needs special care if a witch they were protecting dies. You see, if a witch dies of something other than natural causes, the familiars blame themselves and can go into a deep depression. We have special facilities to care for them and counsel them... bring them to accept the fate of their people and move on to a new witch."

"Oh. That is so sad." I whispered. Swallowing my emotions and turning to Wicked, who was watching the doctor intently.

"This beautiful cat is powerful. I don't think I've ever come across a familiar quite this strong."

Wicked turned her gaze from the doctor and gave me a haughty look, blinking lazily. "Yeah, cat... don't let it go to your head," I warned her with my own superior mien.

"We will meet tonight, then," Adriana confirmed. "This time at my home."

After breakfast, everyone went their separate ways. Adelaide off to make the rounds with a plethora of relatives that came to see her and marvel at her return. June went back to her shop, June's Emporium. Brian and Doctor Clarkston went off to do whatever they needed for their investigation. This left Adriana following me out of the diner and tagging along with me to my studio.

"So. Over breakfast, I thought you might have wanted me here for some specific reason. Am I correct?"

"You are."

"And I assume you didn't want Brian to hear any of what you wanted to tell me?"

"Again... correct."

"So, spill. What did you need to tell me?"

"Not here... let's get inside where there are fewer ears to hear."

Walking into Found Things always gave me a little thrill. My art studio. All my works are lovingly displayed, and projects are waiting to be created. I was just as excited as everyone else in our village with the new fairgrounds almost completed and a place for me to sell my wares. Opening day set for late April had the town was abuzz with the possibilities. We were a folk village that leaned heavily on all things witchy, and this fairground would bring even more business in expanding our village, yet still be just off the square so the shops would benefit as well—a win-win situation.

Climbing to my second-floor loft where my office existed, Adriana and I settled into my comfy club chairs that overlooked the lower level.

"Lorcan did well by you with this place. There is no room on your property to build a studio this big, and you'd probably have had trouble getting permission for it anyway. This is nice." My great-grandmother surprised me with her statement... but I knew she approved of Lorcan and me, even if she teased us un-mercilessly at times.

"So... what's up?"

"Lily?" Lorcan's voice carried throughout the building, and we could hear him rushing up the stairs. He stopped short when he spied Adriana in the opposite chair from me. "Oh, hello, Mrs. Dolce. I didn't expect to see you here."

"I'm glad you showed up. I need both of you to hear my suspicions and then act on them."

Leaning forward a bit, I couldn't help but see how Adriana appeared troubled. Why did I suddenly suspect I'd hate what I was about to hear?

"It's about your mother. I know something about her, and to some extent, you, Liliana, that I fear is something we need to address before anything worse happens than that little performance with Delaney."

"What do you mean? I said I was sorry I lashed out, and I promised to work with Tanaquil to control my temper and harness my dark magic. I know it's not an excuse, but I will master it. I promise." I wrung my hands and felt shame that I drew so much unwanted attention to my family with my uncontrolled antics. Adelaide seemed no better because hadn't she turned those handcuffs to dust?

"No. Lily... let me explain." Lily? Uh oh. Adriana never used my name, always preferring what she thought my parents should have named me.

I listened carefully to what Adriana needed to tell me, but as she began to speak, I was startled to see the ghost of Moira Muir...my grandmother's sister, manifest behind the chair my great-grandmother was sitting in.

"It was no surprise I did not approve of Jessica and Charles getting married." She held up her hand when I opened my mouth to correct her. "I know, I know... we all know the marriage was really between him and Adelaide.

But back then, I was troubled about the match and let my dismay be known. You see. I had always been friends with the Croy clan, which extended to the Muirs and Fortunes. We got along well, and our family would get together with theirs during festivals and such. Moira and I became fast friends, so she let me in on a little secret. Although perhaps that is the wrong word." Moira was nodding her head but kept her focus on the knitting she was doing. I still wondered where a ghost got all that yarn!

"Moira told me the story that was monumental in its confidentiality among that clan. Adelaide telling her tale jarred this memory. You see, they are not pureblood witches." Adrianna stopped speaking as if waiting for me to react. Lorcan drew his brows together but otherwise remained silent. I am sure I looked as confused as I felt.

"So... is this like another Harry Potter moment? Am I part *muggle* or something that purebloods look down on?"

"Liliana, I have no idea of what you are speaking. Muggle? Why must you spout nonsense?" Adriana growled.

"It's a movie reference," Lorcan explained, trying to be helpful.

"Movie? What does that have to do with anything? Pay attention!"

I rolled my eyes and sighed. "Ok... I'm sorry, continue."

"There have always been dark witches in the world, but not with the intensity and power you and Adelaide seem to have in abundance. It is one reason your Aunt Chiara was thrilled when she sensed how powerful you are, Liliana. As strong as I am, I will never be as capable a dark witch as the two of you. If my suspicions are correct, you are even stronger than Adelaide. It was why I had her as an apprentice."

I sputtered at this declaration, knowing how strong Adriana was, but she refused to let me deny her words.

"Let me continue."

I nodded my head, and Adriana told us a tale that left me shocked.

"Far back in your family tree, there was one female relative who didn't belong in the witch world. In her youth, she was renowned for her beauty and excellent singing voice. Even though her kind are considered witches, we did not cross our lines with another Breed, if you will. Their folk has magic, as do we, yet not the same. One of your ancestors became obsessed with this beauty and learned how to get past her dark magic and win her hand. They wed in secret, and her blood has been passed down from generation to generation and with it her dark magic. Strong dark magic, incredibly so. It surpassed anything we had even in the most ancient of families."

Adriana paused, and I shook my head to clear it.

"I don't understand. If this person wasn't a witch, yet she was a witch... just what are we talking about here?" I asked.

"She was a siren. You and Adelaide get your dark magic from her... the Croy and Muir lines... while powerful witches in their own right, never before in recorded history had dark bloodlines in it. You get your dark magic from the sirens. That is why your eyes go black when you call up the darkness."

"Tarni." I quietly uttered the name of the woman I had met at Nichols Pond.

"Yes. Tarni Vanderzee is your cousin."

Just how many flipping relatives would I find popping in and out of my life before all was said and done, anyway? This was getting ridiculous!

"There is more." Adriana continued. "With Charlie mixing his dark witch magical blood with Adelaide's siren magic... they created something of which our paranormal world has never heard. A double dark magical being with powers unknown. You, Liliana, are that great unknown."

"Please tell me I am not going to get hauled off to some witch laboratory and dissected and examined then stored in a jar for future reference?"

"Not unless you get on my bad side. Your grandfather owns a science center that is part of the Dolce Family Trust." She smirked.

I stuck my tongue out at her and blew a raspberry. Lorcan jumped then smiled at me, although he looked worried.

"Then why were you upset when Jessica married Charlie? Or you thought it so."

"I thought, with the three of them living there, in the same house with you, that Addy might accidentally lure Charlie to break his marriage vows. In truth? I didn't want him near any of you for fear of that unknown. I do not know enough about the power sirens hold... no one does."

I glanced at Lorcan and was disturbed to see his frown deepen. Uh oh. Was he changing his mind about me in light of this news?

"Now what?" I was almost afraid to ask the question.

"Now we have to find out what Wilhelmina knows because back before all the horribleness befell this family, Wilhelmina tried to get the Council to halt my training of Adelaide and was petitioning to have an inquest looking into the Croy clan. Her sister Geraldine triggered that memory when I saw her during your fight with Gordon Delaney. Geraldine is much older than Wilhelmina... by almost twenty years, and she was on the Council board that looked into aberrations and tainted bloodlines. I'm afraid they may have found out about the siren blood in your family tree."

"But. Is it illegal or something? To marry outside your... Breed, did you say?" I asked, now understanding the sex magic that popped up unexpectedly a few months back that I'd slammed into Brian, causing him to become dazed. Moreover, it explained Adelaide's bewitching every man with which she comes into contact. Sirens. Gotta love it.

"It isn't usually done. There are no laws against it. But it is frowned upon because it is so rare. The dark magic strain passes down to one heir, it seems. No matter how many offspring the couple has, it seems only one every generation has the siren magic. Therefore, Iona and Jessica did not have it as strong, neither will Nora. Their blood is pure with just traces of siren. It seems an oddity, but that is just it! We do not know enough about sirens because they guard their lore religiously. The same goes for witches... we aren't comfortable sharing information with other Breed.

"How does each Breed then deal with the offspring of such a pairing? Can you imagine a witch mated to a vampire? Or a giant to a siren? More importantly, what does it mean that you have a rare father who is a dark male witch? And a mother who gives you your dark magic through her siren blood?"

I sat pondering these things with Lorcan, who had gone a little green with the news.

Wait. Giants are a thing?

CHAPTER 13

*L*ater that evening, I found myself having a lavish dinner at my great-grandparent's home. My Aunt Iona and Uncle Owen, sans son Douglas who was off on a trip with his friends, were here. As were Aunt Chiara and Uncle Stephen with Andrea and Steve Junior. June, and her son Jake. I was surprised her husband Dennis wasn't with us, but June said he had other things to do. Her words worried me because my friends and I had wondered if Dennis and June were on the outs for a while now. One rumor has it that Dennis had been having an affair with Rita Chase, Brian's mother, but nothing has come of it. Still, to have June leave him out of a family meeting seemed odd, especially since Jake brought Becky.

Lorcan came with his parents, Eileen and Henry, and I was surprised to see his grandfather Malcolm as a guest.

Brian arrived and would hopefully tell us what he discovered about Deputy Gordon Delaney's case. It was weird having him amongst the family again, but after almost losing him last month, things had changed once more, and we had found common ground to move forward. I was glad because even though I had moved past an infatuation and we moved on, he had been good friends to Lorcan, and Jake and I didn't want to be the reason they no longer spoke to each other.

Adriana and Antonio went all out and had prepared a fantastic meal—full-on Italian—with all these wonderful delicacies that had me drooling in anticipation. The lack of staff had me surmising, Granny had done all the work herself, with a little help in the magical department. Even Keisha had a well-deserved night off from her nursing duties, although if anyone else was family around here, she and her aunt Susanne Washington were among them.

Just as I had those thoughts flit through my head, the doorbell rang, and in walked Susanne, but sans Keisha. Instead, her surprise guest left the room speechless.

"Mortimer! How nice that you could come! Please, come in, come in. And you brought Caliente. How nice to see you again, my dear."

Antonio's face lit up when he saw Mortimer again, and he shuffled over to give the vampire a huge hug. It looked like a tiny gnome hugging a sequoia tree, but you could tell Mortimer was touched. Everyone in the room was eying Caliente, Mortimer's lady friend, and I couldn't blame them. Weirder to me was seeing tiny Methodist church lady Susanne, who I recently found out was a lesser witch in the company of the two vampires. My perception was skewed!

After a meal fit for Italian royalty, we all helped clear the table and got down to business, but not before I crammed another arancini in my mouth for good measure.

They were Italian rice balls stuffed with meat, mozzarella, and peas mixed in sauce...the rice was then shaped into a ball, dunked in egg wash, then breaded and deep-fried. Heaven!

I didn't think I could eat another morsel, but Adriana waved her hand across the table, and coffee, tea, and pastries magically appeared. I couldn't believe Mortimer and

Caliente were satisfied with just sipping their wine until I thought about it deeply and came back with the idea that made me queasy... so I just pretended they liked wine and nothing more. Ahem. Moving along.

"Now we get down to business," Adriana stated, rubbing her hands together in anticipation. "We have many things on our agenda and need to come up with a plan of action. One; who killed Gordon Delaney? Brian, I assume you have some news to divulge on this. Two; how do we get into the lower levels of the prison now that the Elders have put guards at the entry and called off all visitation since we found Gordon hanging outside the front door, alerting them to the fact that others know of its whereabouts. Three; what do we do now that I've brought you up to date about Wilhelmina and Geraldine and the siren strain in the Croy bloodline?"

"Four; how is this all tied together, and does it affect our getting my Charlie back," Adelaide uttered softly. The only one in the room not privy to Adelaide being my mother was Malcolm, so he sat back, startled, and was brought up to date with the news.

"I *knew* it. I always knew ye were not just a young lass mooning after yer sister's beau. Why Jess never once showed any sign she was taken by young Charlie. I always thought it odd they wound up married!" He cried.

I just hoped no one else in the village felt the same, speculating at the turn of events, and voiced my concern.

"That's just it!" June worried. "There must be someone who has deliberated then concluded something was not quite right. We know now that the Fredricks girls were gunning after the family, but what about Wilhelmina and her clan?"

Aunt Iona and Uncle Owen shared a look, and I wondered if they were thinking about Nora... and her betrayal.

Brian cleared his throat and took center stage. "We have

yet another mystery on our hands concerning Gordon. It seems he was taken out the same way as Edith, the same as Lily used to remove Yolanda to save Lorcan and the Imperium Tormentum Mortis curse. But this one was different than any other dark spell we've ever come across. Doctor Clarkston said someone channeled the magic through another. How? He could not say. But we need a Tracker...a Shadow Dancer, to find the connection."

If word got out about this or already had... it was no wonder people had been glancing at me surreptitiously. I was one of the only witches able to perform the spell. Martha Mosely...my friend at the library, was another—but no one other than a few people in this room knew that.

Just then, I noticed Edith skulking in the corner and thought it odd she didn't barrel in the room as was her norm.

"Edith? Is everything alright?" I asked the specter.

"No. Everything is just awful. Oh, Lily. My family is horrid. Just horrid! Auntie Geraldine is evil. She has been plotting to destroy your family and seems manic and unbalanced. She keeps her plans from the rest of the family, which means she might be acting alone and hope for the rest of them! I think she is either a dark witch or is working with one! We never had dark witches in our family. That is one of the reasons they are so jealous of yours! How is it she is one?" She wailed and came floating over to my other side.

"My family wants power and prestige and fully intends to take yours down, but I don't think they are playing the same games as Geraldine. My family will go the normal route and scheme and plot how to dethrone you legally. Geraldine has been trying to create her own dark witch line! I saw her notes on Nora and me. She has used dark magic on us for years, trying to create a hybrid witch so our family would have dark magic in it as well. Now she is using Nora as her test subject again since

I'm gone. All those years ago... all those wild college parties. Nora and I had no idea Auntie Geraldine had been plying us with dark magic and using us as an experiment!" Edith began to sob while Adriana retold what she had just heard.

I caught the eye of Caliente Saunders, and the female vampire didn't seem shocked by the news. If anything, she looked excited. Uh oh. What was that about?

"I know I was in my furry prison for twenty years," Adelaide wondered, "but how is it I don't recall this Geraldine person? Who is she in the grand scheme of things?"

Adriana blinked in surprise. "Geraldine is Wilhelmina's older sister, Trouble. You hated her with a vengeance. She was one of your schoolteachers, and you gave her what for! She was one of the reasons your family pulled you out of school and had you apprentice with me."

"Oh! You mean Ms. Dietrich. Of course. You said she was with Nora and Wilhelmina. I didn't see another woman. Certainly not Ms. Dietrich."

"Are you certain?"

"Of course, I'm certain. There were only two women that you sparred with. Wilhelmina and a willowy blonde that must be my niece, Nora. Iona, darling... I am so sorry Nora has chosen to side with a rival family. But Ms. Dietrich? I would think had I seen her, I'd know it. I heard you say Gerry and frowned. I felt like someone was shooting daggers at me but didn't see anyone looking toward me."

"Andrea. Be a dear and fetch me one of Charlie's yearbooks out of the library. They are all in a row to the left of the fireplace. Bottom shelf." Adriana commanded.

Andrea rushed off to gather the item in question, and I watched as Caliente began furiously whispering in Mortimer's ear. He looked confused, then alarmed, then resigned to whatever he was hearing. I wanted to slip over to the duo and question them, but it had to wait as Andrea came back to the dining room with a yearbook in hand.

Flipping through the pages, Adriana paused in the section which listed teachers along with a small bio and photograph. Turning the book so Adelaide could see it, she pointed out Geraldine, much younger and barely recognizable as the woman from the scuffle.

"Yes. That's my old instructor, but she was nowhere around...certainly not with his sister and Nora." Adelaide announced.

"But she was," I spoke up, startling Adelaide, who'd gone pale.

"She couldn't have been... I would have seen her."

"Does anyone have a current photo of the woman?" Becky asked.

We thought a moment, everyone wondering where we'd find such a photo, but then I cried out, "Maureen Kennedy! She was taking photos of our skirmish the other day. She might have one of Geraldine!"

Before you could say get that girl on the phone, quick... June had whipped out her cellphone and began texting furiously. Within minutes we heard the message ding in reply. Smiling with satisfaction, June presented her phone to my mother and said, "there. That's what she looks like now. Time has not been good to her, I'll admit. But she was standing right beside Nora the other day. You must have seen her."

Adelaide took the phone from June with trembling hands and stared at the photo for a long time. Then she turned to Adriana and wailed. "There was no one that looked like this at the scene of the scuffle. But I have seen this woman. She's the old witch I told you about. The one who wanted the talking book back!" Adelaide's voice became shrill. "The very woman who Donna and Deanna befriended and owed their loyalty. Geraldine is behind it all!" she cried, then fainted.

"A shifter. Geraldine is a *shifter*!" Iona cried out, then she, too, collapsed.

"What I want to know is, was I right? Did I see a mermaid swimming in Nichols Pond?" Malcolm asked. Lorcan groaned in response.

"Not now, Grandpa."

After a few minutes of dashing around, getting glasses of water, reviving the two sisters, and then settling down once more to discuss this latest development, we heard a gentle clearing of the throat. Caliente had raised her graceful hand as if asking for the floor.

"If I may?" The beautiful vampire commanded our attention. Her long hair hanging straight down in a cascade of blood-red locks that matched her lipstick and nails once more, she had us enthralled by her very voice, so sultry and enigmatic.

"I am about to shock everyone in this room, and I pray these delicate souls prepare themselves for the information I am about to impart." She glanced at Iona and Adelaide—the elder sister looking grateful for the warning, but Adelaide looking miffed to be deemed delicate.

Caliente continued, "The woman on the phone cannot be Geraldine Dietrich. This is impossible."

"Of course, it's Geraldine Dietrich! I've known her my entire life!" Adriana proclaimed.

"Be that as it may, this woman is not she. For you see, twenty-seven years ago, I killed Geraldine Dietrich when she tried to murder a child of our people in a raid that we have kept secret—lest it destroys the tenuous relationship enjoyed between the witchfolk and vampire.

"Geraldine, and five other witches, stormed our hidden lair where younglings live away from the light of day until they become strong enough to bear the rays from the sun...why they came to destroy children, we still have never discovered. We lost four younglings that day before we managed to kill those responsible. Only one witch was made aware of this horrible incident, Olivia Ogden-Meyers. She was there on behalf of the Elder witch leader... Antonio Dolce, acting as his representative."

We all sat back in collected shock. No one more so than Brian Chase...seeing as Olivia is his great aunt. The only sound that followed was that of the set of false teeth popping out of Grandpa Antonio's mouth as they hit the table in front of him.

CHAPTER 14

*A*ndrea, Lorcan, Jake, Becky, Brian, and I were back at my place. Adelaide had gone to Iona's house intending to spend the night with her sister. After another hour of discussion and finding out Grandpa Antonio not only remembered the event but ordered an inquest, Brian had no choice but to contact his great aunt. She agreed to meet us at Adriana's.

Because of the severity of the incident and the clandestine investigation afterward, Olivia agreed to have Brian use his Veritum ability to test the truth behind her words. To prove his honesty because they are related, Brian also hooked her up to a lie detector test... mundane for the witch world, but the only way to prove he wouldn't lie to protect his aunt.

Olivia passed with flying colors.

The verdict? She didn't see Geraldine Dietrich among those they killed that day. She was shocked to hear Caliente slew her, thinking, as did everyone before this knowledge, that Geraldine had been alive and well and living in a small cottage on the Plank compound here in Sweet Briar or off on one of her many months-long journeys around the world.

Geraldine, after retirement, had become something of a world traveler.

Olivia personally recorded each individual's death and sealed their records, informing their relations of the crimes but not the specifics. The files were locked in a high-security chamber where such records were stored. Caliente assumed Geraldine was among the bodies removed, but because of personal involvement—one of the young vampires who'd lost their lives had been a daughter to a close friend—she had removed herself from the scene once they had neutralized the attackers.

Caliente deduced Geraldine was among the fallen.

The only possibility we could come up with was that Geraldine died and her body had somehow been removed from the scene before Olivia got there, and a shifter assumed her identity all these years. Caliente was positive she'd killed Geraldine...she had no doubts, for she knew her personally but wouldn't go into details. This means someone engineered the attack and was in the chamber to either conceal or remove the remains then take on Geraldine's image all these years. The vampires usually stayed in their dominion, and there was not much interaction, so whoever did the switch didn't worry Caliente would discover this ruse.

That left one possibility and only one. We were dealing with a very powerful shifter. After all, Geraldine's own family couldn't see past the enchantment. That this was well-orchestrated and had multi-levels of deviousness had everyone tense.

The fact that all of us saw an older woman who looked like Geraldine standing with Wilhelmina, including her niece, my ghost, Edith, was beyond disturbing. Only a shifter of high caliber could pull that off—and appear invisible to Adelaide simultaneously? Shocking. This witch shifter mutant of a woman was beyond dangerous.

Despite the lateness of the hour, none of my crew was even remotely tired. We were lounging in the den discussing the day's events and wondered what our next course of action would be. It was nice to see Brian involving us in his case, but at this point, what else could he do? All roads pointed back to my family drama.

"I thought it weird that female vampire wouldn't tell us how she knew Geraldine before the attack." Andrea wondered, looking to see if the rest of us agreed.

Jake was nodding yes, and Becky spoke up for them both, "We did as well. Why not tell us how they were acquainted?"

Brian ran his hand through his hair in exasperation, sighing, He rested his head back on the sofa cushion. "I know why. My aunt told me tonight when she was leaving. Caliente had befriended the witches that attacked their younglings. Geraldine was their leader. They pretended it was an educational research project, and since Caliente knew Geraldine was a teacher, she trusted the woman. Deceived by them all, she paid a huge price for believing what we now know is a rogue group. Can you imagine how she feels realizing she was partially responsible for the death of four young vampires?"

"But it wasn't her fault! How could she have known they planned such a heinous act?" Andrea cried.

"Dre, this was almost thirty years ago... today we have a solid relationship with vampires. Back then? Things were tense." Jake informed my cousin. "If her clan found out she engineered the meeting and allowed the witches entry into the younglings chamber? One of her own would have destroyed her."

"Can she be trusted?" Becky asked.

"Who? Caliente?" Brian queried, "If Mortimer Snodgrass vouches for her, I, for one, have no issue with her. Neither did any of our elders."

"Why didn't you just use your Veritum ability on her?" I asked.

Everyone chuckled as Lorcan answered, "No blood. It's not just the breath as one speaks that Brian uses to detect a lie, but the changes in the blood. Brian can tell by a change in blood pressure, increased heart rate, vasoconstriction, and elevated stress hormones if someone is lying. All play a part. Vampires have no blood remaining in their system—one reason they need to replenish it so often unless they are hibernating—therefore, Brian can't get a reading on them."

Handy trick.

"Well, I guess we know who killed Gordon Delaney." I proposed.

More nods in the affirmative.

"I'm just glad that evil, whatever she is retired before we had her as a teacher!" Andrea cried, then shivered.

"How are we going to inform the Plank's there is an imposter in their midst? I mean, won't they resist our revelations? I can't imagine they will be remotely pleased." I grumbled.

"They won't believe you." Edith manifested over by the mudroom and startled Wicked, who arched, then walked over to sniff the wispy ectoplasm that comprised Edith's lower half.

"Edith says they won't believe us. And why would they?" I stated.

"Especially since no one can get a shifter to transform unless they know what will hurt them. In Mortimer's case, being half-vampire, it's silver. But with this entity? Who knows what is needed." Brian added.

"She looks like such an unassuming old woman." I wondered, "I didn't even take a look at the yearbook to see what she looked like at a younger age. Or what Geraldine looked like anyway."

"Your parents had their yearbooks in the office. Remember when you were sorting that room out? Why don't you fetch one." Edith suggested. I told my friends what Edith said then went and retrieved my mother's. Jessica had her yearbook on the shelf as well, and I moved them to a prominent place in my office because I wanted to take the time to go through them thoroughly and learn who my parents and aunt were before everything changed. With Adelaide back, it had slipped my mind.

Settling back down on the sofa between Lorcan and Brian—and wasn't that slightly awkward—I began flipping through the book to the teacher section, then stopped when I found Geraldine's name, bio, and photographs.

"Whoa. Geraldine looks familiar. I think I've seen this woman somewhere before!"

"It can't be so, Lily. You've never lived here as an adult, and you would have been too little to remember someone you'd hardly have run across when you were here." Andrea exclaimed.

"No. It's more recent. I could swear this face is familiar. But who?" I began running an internal Rolodex of sorts hoping to jog my memory as to where I might have seen the woman. She did look a bit like the old lady I met with Wilhelmina and Nora... but the age difference was off.

"Did the woman on the street seem ancient, Lorcan?" I asked my boyfriend.

"Ancient? No. I would say early sixties, maybe."

"But that can't be. She appeared to be closer to Adriana's age!"

"No way." Lorcan contradicted me.

We all concluded that this shifter must be projecting different images to different people and no image at all to Adelaide. How incredible.

The woman in the yearbook was attractive with an hour-glass figure and a platinum blonde bob. However, her smile seemed cold if a bit superior, and she reminded me of the Cheshire Cat. She instantly had me feeling like a mouse, and I would have hated to be in her classroom. Upon closer inspection, I could even see that she wore cat-eye framed glasses but had them on a chain around her neck.

Wait a minute!

Platinum blonde, curvy, cat-eye frames! Holy Batman in tights! It was Babs! A slightly younger-looking version of the secretary who worked for my mother's attorney! Mister Pearce has a doppelgänger Geraldine working for him named Barbara! Everyone jumped when I shrieked in my eureka moment. But... hang on a minute. How could there be two women so incredibly similar, and it is a coincidence?

I am not big on coincidences—and with good reason!

I hurriedly told my friends what I'd discovered then grabbed my cell phone calling the one person who might be able to help me solve this puzzle.

"Molly! Lily... how are you? Great. Good... good to hear. Well, as a matter of fact, I do need you to do something for me. Is there any way you can go to my mother's attorney and secretly snap a photo of his secretary, Barbara? What!? When?!? HOW!??"

After a few more minutes of hearing what Molly had to say, then promising I'd call her back soon, assuring her the information she just gave me didn't have anything to do with my situation—in other words, I lied—Molly hung up. I turned to my awaiting friends to tell them the news.

"Molly just told me ten days after I returned to Sweet Briar, someone assaulted Mister Pearce, my mother's attorney. After several clients could not reach him on the phone or at his office, they called in the police to investigate. The police found him dead behind his desk. She said it looked like someone bashed him from behind then tore his place apart. She insisted she sent me the news clipping of the incident... but I swear I'd remember if that turned up in the mail. I mean, I haven't kept in touch with Molly these last six months as I promised, but once I found out I lived in the paranormal world, I thought it best to cut ties and keep our relationship to the occasional card or letter."

"Does she really look like this Barbara?" Lorcan asked, putting his arm around me to calm my nerves.

"Identical. I mean, this woman is slightly younger in appearance, but Barbara could be an older sister."

"That means the shifter more than likely killed the real Barbara and took on her persona," Jake said.

"That's just it... Molly said they found Barbara dead in the ladies' room, strangled. She's sending me a photo from the obituary by text."

A ding sounded telling us the text had come through, and for the second time today, I was looking at a woman who had no resemblance to the person I was expecting to see. "This is not Barbara. Not the Barbara I knew anyway. While blonde, this woman is kind of frumpy and plain. My Barbara... or rather... the shifter's Barbara was the spitting image of Geraldine Dietrich!"

"We need to tell the folks, and you need to inform the sheriff, Brian," Lorcan stated.

Brian looked a bit haunted and stood up quickly. "I need to warn the sheriff, you mean."

We glanced at each other, wondering what Brian meant. He hurriedly pulled his phone out of his jacket and began punching in numbers.

"What is it, Brian. What do you know?" I asked.

"Sheriff Buford informed me he was going to have a meeting tonight with the Elders in charge of the prison. In all the fuss today, it must not have dawned on the other Elders —your Uncle Owen and Aunt Chiara, Lily."

"What did they miss?"

"The Elder in charge of the prison... the only one who is aware of the location of the entrance of the prison, the only one who holds the key other than the guards, is Gloria Stillwell."

"Wait. No. Adriana knew where the entrance was. That's how we came to be at the exact spot where Gordon was left hanging." I cried.

"Lily. The entrance location is magical. It changes every day. Just because Adriana knew where it was yesterday doesn't mean she knows where it is today. Gloria met Adriana at the town square, and she told her where the next entrance would be. We will have to contact Gloria again to find out where it has since moved. We also need to make sure Gloria is alive and well... because Geraldine could have done something to her and tricked Adriana."

We sat in shocked silence for a good three minutes. Then Brian turned to me.

"Lily, with you being a Shadow Dancer... and a powerful dark witch, I need you to be the one to track the remnant spell leftover from the Imperium Tormentum Mortis curse. I need to know if it leads to an unknown. Because it won't belong to Geraldine Dietrich, I can guarantee that."

"But I'm not fully trained. I can't." I protested.

"Lily, you must try. I can call Tanaquil, and she can assist you. I will contact her now and have her meet us. She can assist, but only you can do this."

"Why? Tanaquil is a Shadow Dancer as well. Can't she track the magic?"

It wasn't that I didn't want to try. I didn't want anything to go wrong, and we lose the trail... have it run cold. Or worse, have the culprit slip away because I didn't have what it took to perform such spell-crafting.

"Because you have met the woman in New York State

who was supposed to be Barbara... and you have met the woman here that should be Geraldine Dietrich. You've met them both. Your magic will connect the two when you perform your tracking spell. You're the only person who can do this!" Brian proclaimed.

"Please tell me Gordon's body hasn't gone to the Soule's?"

My only answer was an apologetic grimace.

You have *got* to be kidding me!

CHAPTER 15

Chester and Hester Soule—sounds like ghoul—are Sweet Briar's brother and sister team of undertakers. They are an odd duo in a creeptastic way. Seriously. Chester is tall...like touching Mortimer's height tall, and he had an unfortunate habit of standing too close. Way too close. He looks like a science experiment gone horribly wrong. His neck is stretched to epic proportions making it too long for his body, almost like the Kayan Lahwi tribe in Myanmar, whose women put rings around their necks to lengthen them. It also appeared someone might have tried to sew Chester's body parts on. Nothing matched in length, and he had an odd gait that gave him a puppet-like mien. A Mister Bean, in puppet form if you will. He also had an overbite to beat all overbites, tempered by a mustache that looked like a fuzzy caterpillar took up residence on his upper lip.

Hester, his sister, was as short as Chester was tall and as wide as a hippo who came off a binge-eating frenzy after being on Jenny Craig for two months. Picture a creampuff with a chubby face and arms on stick-thin legs. She was forever measuring anyone she came across to size them up properly for one of their coffins. Coffin, mind you. Never say casket around the pair—they only dealt in coffins. Dracula stamp-of-approval coffins. If you don't know the difference between the two, look it up online.

The siblings had just returned from a trip to Nevada, having discovered a couple who lived an hour or so outside Las Vegas that had a ranch called Coffinwood. An off-the-beaten-path attraction where everything is coffin-shaped goodness and skull art wowza. Six-sided old-school coffins were de rigueur, and they even boasted a pet cemetery and wedding chapel—weird Nevada at its best. I knew Mortimer desperately wanted to pay a visit. Who knows? Maybe we'd make a road trip out of it one day and grant his wish.

Unfortunately, Chester had a bit of a crush on me and was delighted when I walked in the door to his realm, giving him a jaunty little salute as I pushed through the swinging doors. Brian and Lorcan were with me, and I was grateful for their company—I hated being in the basement of the frigid funeral home. Hester was nowhere in sight, but I kept my ear out for her tape measure.

Wicked insisted on coming with us, despite my repeated attempts to lock her in the house. I finally gave up, throwing my hands in the air when she managed to slip out the back door after my three tries of tossing her back in and running. On my last endeavor, not only did she move faster than me, escaping into the yard, but she also managed to open my Jeep and sat waiting in the driver's seat with an eat poop grin on her furry face.

Sometimes you had to know when to choose your battles.

"Welcome, welcome! Pleasant to have you visit my humble establishment." Chester gushed as he leaned down to take my hand. "Charmed, I'm sure."

Why did the man always smell like a cheeseburger?

"That's all he eats, sweetie." Hester tittered from behind me.

"Gah!"

I hadn't heard her sneak up behind me and spun around to forestall the inevitable measuring she'd try to sneak in. That I had yet to successfully block the demented duo from reading my thoughts was another reason I hated coming here.

Snap!

"Sixty-three inches, give or take... I'd suggest a seventy incher. More room for fluffy pillows and the like." Chester grinned at the room in general. "Although she'd fit in a sixty-eighter."

"I do not need a casket!"

"Coffin."

Coffin! Casket, pine box... I do not need one and won't for the foreseeable future, thank you very much!" I screeched.

"Oh, no, dear. Never a pine box. Beetles, you know... and slugs. Worms even. And caskets! Well, no one wants an exploding casket for their loved one." Hester stated primly.

"Exploding caskets? I don't even. Enough with the coffin talk."

"Casket. If one is speaking of exploding casket syndrome, then it's a casket. That's why we only use coffins." Hester continued.

"There is no such thing as exploding casket syndrome... I'm sure you..." I stopped speaking when Chester whipped out his cell phone, showing me an article on exploding casket syndrome.

Huh. Who knew?

I crossed my arms and tapped my foot.

I could tell Lorcan and Brian were holding back grins and shot them a surly look. Both of them rushed back out the swinging doors into the hallway, but it didn't stop the sound of laughter one bit. The only thing that stopped me from chasing after them and reading them the riot act was the entrance of Tanaquil Alessi.

"Children. Let's get a move on if you please. Good morning Hester, Chester." Tanaquil was all of four feet tall and looked like a porcelain doll or a dainty fairy. She was slim and delicate and could probably pass as a child if it weren't for the wizened gaze which detracted from her youthful appearance, her eyes harboring an old soul. She also bore an uncanny resemblance to Reba McEntire, which always had me doing a double-take when we crossed paths.

Tanaquil as my past dark arts instructor and someone I looked up to, had my nerves easing slightly. In my world of wacky family, crazy happenstance, and magic and mayhem galore, Tanaquil was often the respite I needed, and I sought her counsel, often.

"Shall we?" Chester clasped his hands together then began rubbing them in anticipation. I felt squeamish but refused to appear weak, especially in front of the men.

"Apple?" Hester held out one of the tiny red fruits under my nose, causing me to squeak with its sudden appearance. "Good for one's tummy if one feels ill, you know."

"No, thank you. Let's just get this over with."

Chester escorted us into the next room, where Gordon Delaney lay under a white sheet. Only his head and feet were visible. I hoped I wouldn't have to see him completely naked to get a read with my Shadow Dancer tracking ability. Trackers could trace magic and use it for hunting someone lost or on the run, among other things. A Shadow Dancer was the highest form of Tracker and extremely rare. Lucky me. I just happened to be adept at it... or so everyone thought. We shall see.

Suddenly, the room plunged into darkness. I let out a

small *"meep"* before a spotlight came shining down on where Gordon lay stretched out on the metal gurney. Music began to play softly, something atmospheric and ambient sounding. It would be better suited to an acupuncturist office or aromatherapy shop.

Hester began digging around in a cabinet drawer and whirled around when she found the object with which she'd been searching. It looked similar to my Oculus Rod. It was smaller and unadorned, but there was no denying the shape and glass on either end... although I suspected this one would not share kaleidoscopic duality as did mine.

"Here you go! Get ready for the show!" Hester giggled, handing it over.

"What do I do?" Turning to Tanaquil, I ran my teeth across my lower lip and gazed at her in worry.

"First of all, relax, Lily. Open yourself to the call of darkness and breath out your sensory magic. You have done this before. You can do it again." Tanaquil's soothing voice gave me enough confidence to do as she suggested, and I was pleasantly amazed to find the magic to answer my call.

"Now, send out your Tracking feelers and gaze through the lens. You have done something similar to this, but this time you are tapping your Shadow Dancer skills."

I peered through the lens at Gordon's face, which was tinted a grayish-blue. The old adage struck me as funny when I noticed he looked as if he were sleeping... let sleeping dogs lie. So, I snickered, trying to control my rampant emotions. Pressing my lips together, I concentrated on my task. At first, nothing much happened. But then I began to notice a faint green ooze that seemed to mix with a sparkling orange essence. I went up and down the length of his body—thankfully still under the sheet—but I couldn't figure out why there were two colors.

"There is an orange film present. I believe it is the magical trail we are seeking. But there is also a green mist that I'm sure I've seen before but can't remember where."

"Pull the orange stream into this vial, dear. I don't see it. Please bring it to you and let it flow into the bottle. Then when you have all of it, place the stopper on top. Close it tightly." Tanaquil instructed.

Once I had this task completed, I stepped a bit closer to the body and tried to figure out what the greenish mist that encompassed it was. That is until Gordon Delaney's ghost sat up and said, "Lily... you can see me?"

"Oh no! No. *No... no... no... no... no!* Just, NO!" I stomped my feet with every negative utterance and flapped my arms for emphasis. "I am *NOT* going to be haunted by another ghost—especially this ghost! I'm not!"

I held my palm out to Gordon, who was looking between Lorcan, Brian, and me. He seemed confused and a touch angry.

Why me?

* * *

"DON'T. Just do not ask me to question Gordon. I don't even like him. I thought Edith would be a horror to have around. This is too much to ask of me!" I crossed my arms and marched over to my Jeep, leaning against it, and looked anywhere but at the two men and the spectral form standing near them.

Wicked was under my Jeep growling and puffed up with her tail going a mile a minute. See? Sometimes we were in accord. This was one of those times.

"Lily. Please just ask Gordon what he knows. What happened to him. Then I am sure he will move on to wherever he is supposed to move on to." Brian begged me.

"Oh, really? And what happens if he stays stuck to me like

the other two ghosts at my house? Huh? Are we supposed to take him on our honeymoon, Lorcan?"

"You guys are talking marriage?" Brian gave Lorcan a blank look, and he responded with a sheepish shrug and began to pull at his ear.

"Hello? Can we focus on me here? What am I supposed to do about this?"

"We haven't specifically mentioned marriage, but we agree we are on the same path in life, and I can't imagine being anywhere without her by my side," Lorcan replied.

"Why don't you just have sex with her already so I can get some answers here!" Gordon shouted. Since I was the only one who could hear what he'd said, I opened my mouth in shock and took in too much air, too quickly, and began to cough.

"Do not mention sex and try to rattle me you, you..."

"You've gone there already?" Brian was shocked and gave Lorcan an appraising look.

"What? No... I mean, it's... we..." Lorcan stumbled over his words, and I had just about had enough of this talk.

"That is nobody's business but ours: Lorcan and mine. And for your information, the closest we got to anything like that was seeing Lorcan strip off his shirt and having to pause what I was saying while a mild fantasy moment ran through my mind. Other than that, we have just gone on a few dates! Honestly... what is it with you men and sex?" I screeched.

"You got distracted by my naked torso? Did you think about sex?" Lorcan asked.

"Stop saying sex!" I hollered.

Seeing as how we were standing on the sidewalk outside the funeral home diagonally across the street from A Tale of Two Witches Tea Shoppe, I was horrified when my voice carried like an echo right through the front door. This caused Hermione and Hortense to rush out in a hurry to see what all the fuss was.

"Did someone mention sex?" Hortense cried, then simpered when she noticed Brian and Lorcan standing by me. "Sister dear, look... it's Lily, and I believe she is fighting over which man she intends to bed. Or are you planning a ménage à trois?"

"Whoa! Take it down a notch, ladies. There is a huge misunderstanding here... and please don't go around spreading that rumor, or I will never live it down. I just innocently mentioned the word marriage, and everything suddenly went..."

"Marriage! You and Lorcan? Oh! I knew you two were dating!" Shrieked, Hermione and I groaned when I heard her voice echoing in the opposite direction.

Wait. *What?* How could she know Lorcan and I started anything?

"You must have your wedding shower here at the shop. We'd love to host it, and I suggest a spring wedding because just think of all the flowers we will have sprinkled around the place! Will you be wearing pure white?"

Of all the...

"Ok. Stop it. Right now. There is no wedding. There isn't going to be a wedding. This has all been a misunderstanding, and I really need to concentrate on murder... not marriage, right now!"

"Lily, dear. Men aren't going to be pleased with your little side hobby, even if they are witches. You have entirely too much fun looking into murders. It isn't proper for a young lady." Hermione tsked.

"I'm a flipping dark witch, for heaven's sake! Half the things I do aren't proper!"

"Not with that attitude. It's very unbecoming." Hortense sniffed.

I stood there with my mouth hanging open, almost assured of the fact that drool was pooling in my mouth, ready to dribble down my face. I snapped my trap shut and pinched my fingers between my eyes as if warding off a headache.

"Weren't you the one who mentioned a ménage à trois? How can anything I say be more upsetting to you? Now, if you don't mind, I need to sort out something far different than a ménage à trois!"

"A ménage à trois only works if you lay down some ground rules aforehand."

"Abner! How did you? Ok, that's it. I'm finished."

I scooped a protesting Wicked up, tossing her into my Jeep, then stomped around to the driver's side and promptly fell flat on my face when I felt a bolt of magic slam into me from behind.

* * *

"TRY SOME MORE TEA. Hurry, Hortense! Oh, look... she's coming to." I heard Hermione fussing as the fog lifted from my head, and I tried to sit up. I surmised someone had carried me into the tea shop since I'd been lying flat in one of the deeply cushioned booths.

"No more tea! And please stop shouting. I feel like my head is splitting in two." In fact, my shirt was so damp from the ministrations I received. It looked like they were trying to bathe me in it instead of pouring tea down my throat. I was soaked.

I heard a jingle as someone came into the store and heard Adriana before seeing her since I had a hoard of people in my face.

"Move out of the way. Come on, pronto! I have a business

with Liliana! Ah, cara. You're looking better. I hear congratu-
lations are in order!"

She did *not* just go there.

"Listen, you old bat. Don't start in about my wedding
plans or lack thereof. Not now!"

"Who said anything about wedding plans? I was going to
congratulate you on your upcoming threesome, but if you
want to go the old, boring marriage route, it's fine by me."
Adriana sniffed.

"Argh!"

"Now look what you've done. Lily's aura has gone all dark
again." Hermione clucked.

I started pulling my hair but stopped when I noticed the
little silver box from my mantle sitting on the table in front
of me where my great-grandmother placed it.

"We forgot to open the box!" I cried.

"Yes. We forgot to open the box, which has me highly
upset. I must be slipping in my old age. It took me an hour to
go through all your dirty laundry to find the key tucked in a
pocket of your jeans. You need to get better at housekeeping,
Squirt. Especially if you are getting hitched... men expect a
trade-off, and laundry is one of them."

Lorcan and Brian were wedged into a booth behind me
and struggled to be the first round to my side. Shooing my
granny to have her make room, Brian took the seat next to
her while Lorcan sat by me.

"I guess we know who the victor is then." Adriana cackled
wickedly.

"Wicked! I left her in the Jeep!"

"Really? You think she'd stay there. She's behind the
counter, lapping up a dish of fresh cream." Adriana replied.
"Now. What did the magic feel like? Was it dark? Did it spread
once it hit you? Did you lose all sound before you blacked out?"

I sat a moment thinking hard, then shook my head which I immediately regretted since it made me instantly nauseous.

"I think it felt almost like I went numb, like when you hit your funny bone? That sensation, but all over and then numbness until everything went dark."

"It sounds like she was hit with a Return to Me spell," Brian said.

"What's that? No... wait! I remember. It's a spell that calls to something that belongs to you, even if someone else has it."

"Brava, cara. Good. Do you see? You are starting to remember everything you've learned. You are correct. I believe you were attacked by you-know-who, and she was trying to get her essence back. Lucky for us, Tanaquil snuck out the back way and transported the vial to her lab. Unfortunately for you, you got the brunt of the attack."

"I feel fine, though. I think."

Lorcan put his arm around me, pulling me close. "Please don't ever go running off like that in anger. I don't deserve it, and you don't either. That temper of yours is getting lively. I'm going to have to change your nickname to Etna... or Vesuvius!"

I felt the tension and pain, the last vestiges of the spell drain away with Lorcan's touch, and I leaned into him.

"If you wouldn't rile me up so, I wouldn't need to get lively! And Abner! Where did he run off to?"

"Hey, can't blame Abner this time. He was walking toward us with his lunch in hand, and you came flying out of the funeral home and almost knocked him off his feet. Didn't you see him?" Brian laughed.

"See him? All I could see was that lousy ghost, and that made me see red!"

"How dare you bother my friend!" Edith shouted.

"Friend? You hated her just about as much as I do. Now

she's your friend?" The ghost of Gordon Delaney was nose-to-nose with my spectral houseguest, and now the duo started arguing in the tea shop.

"I used to hate her. Now she is my dear friend, and I won't have you bothering her!"

"Oh, you're going to stop me, are you?" Gordon shouted.

"Yes! Yes, I am!" Edith screeched then began slapping Gordon, who tried to block her advance, only her hands were going through his ectoplasm, and his arms kept puffing into swirls of smoke as he tried to avoid her.

"Anyone taking bets?" Adriana quipped.

"This is getting old. I can't keep collecting ghosts. I'm going to have to get a bigger home!

Hortense came over with another cup of tea which she placed down in front of my great-grandmother. "Toten Schweigen-geist!"

Suddenly, both Edith and Gordon froze in place before zapping out of existence.

"What did you do to them?" I cried. Hoping Hortense hadn't done some kind of spell that made Edith disappear forever. Whoa. Wait a minute. What did I care if she did? Yet, I found myself watching and hoped Edith was ok.

"Relax. I sent Edith back to your house to cool her heels and Gordon back to the cold slab he'd been lying on!" Hortense informed me.

Wow. That was some handy spell. Even Adriana looked impressed.

"German?" She asked.

"Yes," Hortense replied. "Daddy always had us learning our spells in the old language."

"Nice."

Hortense trilled a little laugh behind us as she wandered back over to Hermione, who was now feeding Wicked sardines—definitely spoiled, that cat.

147

"Why did you bring the box here? How did you know... forget it. Grapevine. Anyway, why did you bring it to me here?" I asked.

"Because I went to your place to see if you'd returned and found Adelaide instead. She was heading out to meet up with Becky, who ordered a new book, Shifter Lore. It arrived this morning."

"She was able to order a paranormal book about shifters?" I was amazed at this news.

"Amazon. You can find anything on there." Adriana stated, leaning forward.

"While I was there, that box began to glow. It gave me the sense that it was imperative you open it immediately... so here I am. Open it."

"What, now? Here?" But what if a public place was not secure enough to keep whatever is inside a secret? Adriana just nodded her head, and Brian and Lorcan drew close like a protective shield surrounding me.

I used my pointer finger to draw the key toward me, then picked it up. Next, I picked up the silver box and carefully placed the key in the keyhole—a perfect fit. Turning the key, I stopped when I heard a tiny click sound and the box lid popped open. All four of us stared at the blood-red gem ring surrounded by diamonds. It was an emerald cut ruby, the likes of which I had never seen before, set in silver. So intense was the color red, so deep and rich like a drop of blood, I almost questioned its authenticity. It was real; however, there was no doubt of it due to the brilliance and clarity of the diamonds and the sheer beauty, not to mention power emanating from the center stone.

I reached out to remove it from the box, but Adriana stayed my hand.

"Don't touch it." My great-grandmother had grown so

pale. I worried that she might be under a spell of some kind or felt ill.

"What is it? What's wrong? Are you feeling poorly?" Lorcan asked.

"That's one of the familial jewels my grandfather filched." She whispered in a weakened voice. "And I don't know how Charlie came to have it."

If ever there was a time for doomsday music to begin to play, this was it.

CHAPTER 16

I'd like to say the entire family convened at my place to discuss this disturbing bit of news. However, all that happened was Adriana closing the box and having me rush home with it, making me promise to hide it behind the loose brick we'd discovered in my fireplace.

I'd also like to report we figured out our next move, but instead, three entire days went by and not a word from Adriana. She told me to hang around the house, not let Adelaide wander too far, and keep the contents of the box a secret.

I felt like Bilbo Baggins awaiting the return of Gandalf the Grey... only I had absolutely no urge to try on that ring any time soon. Once I heard it belonged to a Romano, I knew I wanted no part of it.

How the heck did my father come by it? Wasn't it bad enough it was a stolen item and probably had bad mojo? What if it belonged to the very two who sent an assassin to poison their son, Marcus' wife, Amelia? Marcus then came to America with their only child, Luigi, who married Elisabetta and had my great-grandmother Adriana. The ring must have somehow continued down to Antonio Junior and then son, Charles... and now to me. But how?

Obviously, dark magic was afoot, so, for once, I heeded what Adriana had said, and remained home. Sometimes it makes sense to hide under the blankets at least until you had more information and knew how to proceed.

"I'm making pancakes, I think," I said as I stretched lazily in bed. Wicked was draped across the top of my head, purring and drooling a bit, and chose not to listen. "Perhaps I will make some bacon and slip you some."

Yawning loudly, Wicked rolled over and off my head, down to my chest, where she sat up and stared at me.

"Oh, bacon is what floats your boat. Well, maybe I will make some since you are so complacent now." Wicked scrunched down, then launched off my chest and onto the window seat, where she batted at the lock until it opened, slipping out onto the roof.

Or not.

"I'm going to lock you out someday. Then what will you do?" Probably slide down the gutter or float across the yard. I give up when it comes to that cat and her magical ways.

I was staying in my pajamas, because why not? I ambled down the stairs and into the kitchen, following the scent of fresh-brewed coffee. Adelaide was sitting in the sunporch looking through a magazine and smiled when she looked up and saw me.

"Good morning, darling. How did you sleep?"

"Like I had a cat on my head all night. You?"

My mother laughed and pulled me in for a hug. Something she had never seemed to tire of doing since her return. I had to say I liked every bit of her affection but found myself comparing her to Jessica, which made me feel guilty. How different the two sisters were. Jessica not demonstrative in the least and always sullen and scared. Adelaide was forever reaching out to hold me or touch me and constantly laugh at one thing or another.

Noticing my unease, my mother pulled the chair out beside hers and ordered me to sit.

"Let me get you some coffee, and then we can discuss those pancakes with the side of bacon you promised Wicked. I haven't had pancakes... well, since Deanna turned me. But I haven't forgotten how to make them!"

"How did you know what I told Wicked?" I asked in wonder.

"Because I suddenly had the urge to make them, plus she just flew past the window with a *"mreow,"* so I knew you'd be soon to follow. Mind if I add orange juice to complete the meal? Or do you prefer apricot? I bought some yesterday. Oh, and we have to add this powder. Adriana concocted a spell that will make it easier for us to spot a shifter posing as another. It's not foolproof, but it's close. She's made enough for the entire village. Joe is adding it to his coffee, and so is your Uncle Stephen. The Winters will do the same with their tea orders. Soon everyone should be fairly safe."

No wonder I haven't heard from Adriana.

"Now, what will it be... orange or apricot?"

This domestic bliss was surreal. Here I was. Sitting in my sunroom with the woman who gave birth to me, yet we were strangers of a sort. I suddenly became angry at everything and everyone, especially those responsible for what had happened to my family.

"Oh, here now. What is it? What's wrong, Puss?" Adelaide kneeled in front of me, lifting my chin, so our eyes met.

"Puss? How come I remember that somehow?"

"It's what I called you whenever you got angry. Short for Sourpuss. When you were in a good mood, I called you..."

"Tinkerbell." I finished.

"That's right. You loved the stories I would tell you of all the different fairies... but Disney's Tinkerbell was your favorite."

"Lorcan calls me Tink because I tinker making my art pieces."

"And isn't that just the right of it then? You two are meant to be. Kismet." Adelaide smiled and rushed into the kitchen to gather what she needed for breakfast. I trailed behind her.

"Now. Tell me what made you upset. You were smiling one minute, and then your entire face fell into sadness."

"Ad...um. Mother. See? Why did this have to happen to us? I can't even call you mom, or mother or even Adelaide without tripping over the words. It's not fair that you were taken from me! And now... even now, it is so uncomfortable all the what-ifs and whys! I keep feeling like I'm hurting my mother...my...Aunt Jessica, argh! Do you see what I mean yet?" I bawled. Suddenly everything I had been through in the last six months, along with the last two years of nursing an ill mother who turned out to be my aunt, along with the dark evil that is trying to rip this family apart, was too much to bear any longer. I began to sob.

Adelaide, breakfast forgotten, ran over to me and wrapped me up in her arms. She led me to the sofa and began to rock me back and forth. I was so exhausted with all of it that I allowed her to do so and felt myself melt into her embrace.

It was at that moment she began to sing:

Song of fire the love between
In the wind with wings
Call the stars the moon and sun
Tears fall as she sings

Deep her home beneath the sea

Calls her love to bring
But he cannot stay for long
Tears fall as she sings

Promise me you'll be my own
Beyond the life, we lead
Even as her lover falls
He says, "Eternally."

Whisper in the wind, my love
Hold on to my ring
Even as I fade away
Tears fall as she sings,
Tears fall as she sings

I DRIED my eyes with the sleeve of my pajamas and looked at Adelaide in wonder.

"Your voice is incredible. That song, it was beautiful. Haunting and sad."

"Tarni taught me the words and the melody. It's her song of lament." Adelaide said quietly. "It's the siren blood that flows in me... and in you as well, my darling. When you accept the siren song, you too will sing like that."

I laughed a little and pushed myself upright. "Apparently, you've not heard about my abysmal singing voice. Oh... I enjoy belting out a tune, but no one within a mile of my voice can stand it for more than a minute or two." I said self-consciously.

"You will see, Puss. You will see."

"Tell me about her? How did you meet?"

Adelaide sighed, then half-turned to face me. Tarni is our distant cousin, and please do not ask me how our lineage crosses. I know her father is full merfolk, but her mother was half-witch and half-merfolk, and it is through she that we are related. It is a sad tale, but one Tarni needs to tell, for she asked me not to repeat it. I can tell you that her father is a horrible creature and took several wives. Tarni's mother was the fifth. She has one full-blood sister, Kimberly, younger than she. And six older half-sisters. They had a falling out, and Tarni is in an exile of sorts... of her own doing. But again, the tale is for her to tell. I'm glad the two of you met. Perhaps we can try and find her once this mess of ours is settled."

"Can I ask you about the dagger?"

My mother gave me a curious look and nodded yes. I felt a bit foolish hounding her about little details that puzzled me or the whys of what happened so long ago. But the dagger had always intrigued me. So, I asked, "Why the dagger? Why this ornate dagger if an ordinary knife can do the trick and you can make the blood sacrifice for my father?"

Adelaide leaned down and pulled the dagger out of a sheath she had concealed in her boot. *Whoa!* That was kind of badass. Ever since my mother has awakened from her deep sleep, her clothing has gone from simple and comfortable sweats—which we had dressed her in—to rather tough-looking and what I would describe as biker clothing. Picture lots of leather, form-fitting yet flexible. Nothing flashy... more like she means business. If she wasn't wearing those types of outfits, she was stylish goth in shades of purple. Either way, she pulled off the look, and since she could pass for my age, and we were the same size, I wondered if she'd let me raid her closet!

"I think I have a leather jacket with your name on it." She quipped.

"You read my mind!" I groaned. "I've been trying to get better at blocking... but when I'm stressed..."

"You lose focus. I can help you with that." She promised.

Adelaide looked down at the knife and told me its story.

"Your father taught me how to make knives. It was one of

the only hobbies he had other than gardening. I made this dagger when I first became proficient in dark magic. Made of obsidian, I crafted it as a human would, using a flint-knapping technique with lead and copper... but that's where normal crafting ended. Once I formed the blade, I switched to dark magic, added ancient alchemical and elemental magic, and polished it to this glossy finish. Humans used to make blades with flint or obsidian, but when steel came along, everything changed. Even though obsidian can be hewn five-hundred times stronger than steel... it is fragile. With the magic I infused into this blade, that fragility has been eliminated. Virtually nothing can destroy it. Your father was so proud of me when I completed it...he made the sheath to go with it that I'm now wearing.

"I was going to give this to you when you came of age as a witch. I knew, with having double dark magic in you, you'd probably need it."

We both laughed then I quickly sobered as she held it out to me.

"I used this for the ritual because it brought me close to both of you. You can have it now."

"No! Thank you, but... I don't know how to handle knives. I would love this gift. But you still need to do the blood ritual once a month. Maybe if this ever ends, this attack on us, you can show me?"

"When it ends."

"When." I agreed.

Adelaide stood then, replacing the knife in the sheath, and went to return to the kitchen. However, after glancing at the fireplace, she paused. "What is behind that brick? Look, it's glowing!"

"Oh! That is the box Granny had me open. She said my dad hid it down in the cupboard in the forbidden section of the library... and when I opened it, her familial ruby ring, one of the ones stolen by her grandfather, was inside. But she said to... hey! Wait! Stop!"

Adelaide rushed over to the brick and pulled it away, exposing the hiding spot. Grabbing the silver box, she opened it. Before I could reach her, she plucked the ring from its holder then slipped it on her finger.

"No! Don't put it on!"

But it was too late.

As I watched in horror, Adelaide began to disappear. I tried grabbing onto her, but my hands passed right through her image. Looking at me with sad eyes open wide, she slowly faded away.

"*NO!*" I remembered screaming, then falling to my knees as the small 'ping!' of the ring hitting the floor registered. Then I blacked out.

This time I welcomed oblivion.

CHAPTER 17

I heard familiar voices and wondered why I seemed to be lying down with people tucking blankets around me, whispering in frightened voices.

"Do *not* go near that ring!"

I heard Adriana and couldn't figure out why she seemed so agitated. No... that wasn't anger I heard in her voice it was fear. Why is it so important not to touch the ring?

The ring!

"*Mother!*" I screamed even as I sat up, throwing the blankets off me as I looked around the room, hoping it had all been a dream. From the look on the faces of my family and friends, I could see it was not.

"She's gone." Turning to my great-grandmother, I fell into her arms sobbing and told her what had transpired. Adriana held on to me, petting my back all the time, speaking to me in a soothing voice, trying her best to settle my nerves.

"Don't blame yourself, cara. Adelaide knew what that ring was. A portal to the enemy... a direct one. She didn't want you to fight her battles and sacrificed herself before anyone suggested you put it on."

Tanaquil sat down on my other side and waited until I had better control over my emotions. After I cried myself out, she reached for my hand and sent some magic coursing through me that allowed my sorrow to ebb and my panic to fade until I felt maybe not quite myself, but someone who could cope with whatever we had to do next.

"That ring made my mother disappear. She put it on and faded within seconds!"

"Cara. Liliana... we will find her. Don't worry. We will figure out where the magic took her, and we will return your mother to you. I promise."

I glared at Adriana, needed someone to lash out at. "It's your family ring! How can you not know what the magic will take her? Is she dead? Did it kill her?"

I felt rage. I could sense the dark magic calling to me, and I wanted to let it take over. My self-control had me keep it in check, however. At that moment, I knew I had Jessica to thank for my discipline. Adelaide raising me would not have had the same result. I let that discipline go lately, but no more. I had to be in control at all times. Too many people counted on me. I knew that now. I learned it the hard way.

My Aunt Iona was crying in the dining room. Every heartfelt sob ripped through me as if I swallowed barbed wire.

"I'm going to get my mother back."

Tanaquil fought to grab my attention once more and keep it. "Lily. You did well the other day. The essence you traced definitely led us to the shifter pretending to be Geraldine. It was she who killed Gordon Delaney."

"What do I care about that now? Don't you understand I've lost her again? I've lost my mother!"

"Stop it. Remain calm. Don't you understand yet? It was the witch shifter who killed Gordon. It was the same shifter who took on the image of Geraldine and has pretended to be her for decades now...even fooling her family. More importantly, this same witch shifter has been behind it all, conspiring with Donna and Deanna. She fooled Jessica, Adelaide, and Charles with her talking book and lies and the rose. You told Adriana she looked like the woman who worked for Jessica's attorney. Everything is coming from this woman, and you traced the essence, so we have proof!"

"What does it matter now that Adelaide is gone?"

"Not gone. Just missing." Adriana uttered softly.

"This creature is behind all of the destruction to your family. She is the one who tainted the ring... it must belong to her. Your Shadow Dancer power showed us who and what we are fighting. We can battle this woman now." Tanaquil proclaimed.

Andrea ran over to me and dropped to one knee, getting me to look her way. "Lily... if your father hid that box for you to find. He had to know the ring was dangerous. Maybe he needed you to find it for a reason?"

I looked around the room and noticed that everyone involved as of late was present and accounted for. Lorcan, Brian, Jake, Becky and Andrea. Aunt Iona and Uncle Owen. Aunt Chiara minus Uncle Stephen and Steve Junior, who were probably at their café. Mortimer and Caliente stood off to one side. June and Dennis Carter were here as well as Eileen and Henry Reid. Adriana and Grandpa Antonio. Susanne Washington and Keisha Holcomb. Usually, this would give me hope, being surrounded by so many people I loved and loved me in return, but with Adelaide taken, I couldn't get through my pain to figure out what I needed to do next.

"We are preparing for war. Geraldine... or this imposter Geraldine, has disappeared. We confronted Wilhelmina via Olivia Ogden-Meyers, and even she has been suspecting her 'sister' as of late. Nora has been feeding Olivia information, and we have the diary." Adriana stated.

"We need you to focus because we must plan. This is going to happen now, soon. Perhaps... perhaps she has Adelaide, even as we speak. Perhaps they are battling it out right now. Therefore, we must act immediately." Tanaquil informed us all.

"What did this diary say? What did my tracking her essence show." I asked.

"Geraldine, let us call her this, for now. Geraldine ranted on and on about the three, Jessica, Charles, and Adelaide, and how mixing the power would ruin her plans. She wanted to destroy Charles, but not in a way that would end him... but end the family. It sounds as if she knows where he is, but didn't write it down. We know she is aware of some family secrets because she keeps referencing this. But again, she did not write it down. The one thing she did give us a clue on is what she is." Adriana informed me. "And you Shadow Dancer magic proved it."

I felt my interest pique, knowing that we had a way to fight her and win if we had that information.

"What is she?" I asked.

"A changeling," Adriana said darkly.

"What does that mean?" I asked, confused at the word.

"She used to be half-witch, half shifter, but she became a vampire by having herself turned. She is not a true-born vampire... she was made one."

"That means what?"

Mortimer cleared his throat. "If I may? A changeling is weaker than a full-blood vampire. Weaker still than me, full-blooded vampire on one side and full-blooded shifter on the other. A changeling, however, is turned and depends on blood to live as do we, but needs it more. Requires it often and cannot handle long periods in the sun when in vampire state. This changeling is strong in one way, but in vampire, form is very weak. Too many halves make up the whole if you will. To shift our changeling into vampire form requires a simple substance that I believe you are familiar with."

"Silver?"

"Silver."

"That explains why she dressed like a mummy. She was trying to keep from being touched accidentally by silver." I mused.

"Perhaps, but we have something that will take care of that."

"The ring came in a silver box. The ring was set in silver." I stated.

Looking at the box now lying on the floor, my eyes tracked over to the ring.

"What do we do about that, now?"

"I don't know yet," Adriana muttered. "I don't want anyone to touch it for now."

I looked up at Caliente, who stood near it, but far enough away lest the silver on the ring touch her. We made eye contact, and I could tell she wanted to say something to me, but in private. I would wait for an opportune time to slip away and speak with her.

"How do we find her? Geraldine."

"Her last entry in the diary was this morning. She wrote that she'd break the wards on the prison and free Donna and her army." Tanaquil told us, her voice calm.

"Then we need to stop her. That's where she is... that must be where mom is. How do we fight her?"

Brian came over to me and pulled me up off the sofa leading me to the kitchen table. On it was several boxes filled with what looked like silver toothpicks. But much larger than the average toothpick. Lorcan came up behind me and wrapped his arms around me, resting his head on my shoulder.

"These are magical darts. If you hold them in your hand and throw them at your opponent, they will always regenerate unless you switch to your magic. Then you will have to gather the ones you threw down to restart the process. We are waiting on Gloria Stillwell to arrive with news of where we can find the new entrance. She never met Adriana in the park that day. It was the shifter. The fake Geraldine set it up, knowing we were going to show up. She killed Gordon and left him there to stall us until she decided to break the wards. We're running out of time."

I pulled out a kitchen chair and sat down. I was trying to process everything that was coming at me at dizzying speed.

"Will these darts go through any getup Geraldine might be wearing?" I wondered aloud.

"They will go through the toughest hide, the thickest coat... don't worry, I can assure you if you throw them at this shifter, you will make her feel intense pain."

I thought some more, feeling my nerves ease up a bit as the information began making sense.

"How will we know Gloria is Gloria? How do we know who anyone is since this shifter can manipulate features at will? Will your potion work?" I asked Adriana

"It will help, but from now until we nab this evil creature, we touch everyone we meet with the silver. She will have to shift out of her image, even for a second to heal her vampire body, then shift back... or shift into something else." Tanaquil said from behind me.

"So, if I get enough in her, she will go insane having to switch back and forth over and over rapidly. I need to figure out where her weakest spot is and nail her there with these darts. Then I can strike."

"We. We will all be there, helping you."

I sat there for a moment and considered what I'd just heard. Wicked took that time to jump into my lap and paw at my face. I looked down at and she made a soft "mew" sound that broke my heart.

"I miss her too, Wicked. I promise I will get her back."

"Mreow."

$\mathcal{M}$y home turned into a war room. All my friends and family gathered around the dining room table and plotted the next move we should make. Gloria Stillwell arrived, got poked by a dart, passing the test, and told Adriana she was so upset a shifter had managed to worm their way into this village and attack so many families. She asked to stay and help strategize. We allowed her to stay, of course, once we poked her a few more times for safe measure.

Most shifters were docile. A solitary Breed that never posed a danger to others. But occasionally, the paranormal world came across certain creatures that changed into the worst their kind could become. We were dealing with such a creature, like our own little Hitler trying to dominate our world. We were about to show ours the door... to oblivion.

We had all strapped the silver darts to ourselves. They came with a handy pouch to keep them tucked close and give easy access once we needed to use them. Adriana was trying to look through family journals to see who was half-witch and half-shifter in her heritage. Something she found incredulous since she hadn't any idea there *were* any!

Andrea was in my living room with Becky, and they were poring over the diary. They were trying to figure out the last paragraph Geraldine wrote. She mentioned an item she needed to give to Donna so victory would be theirs no matter what we might do.

"I don't get it," said Becky, "the passage kept repeating the line: *Use the ring, and the opposite will always give what you desire.* Another line said: *To break down the wards, deceit is the key. If they find out first, the battle is lost.* The final line of that paragraph was more rantings about the talking book: *Never tell someone to make something so small again it's easy to lose.*"

"What does it mean, though?" said Andrea, "and is she talking about the ring Adelaide had on? I just don't understand," she grumbled.

Adriana listened with half an ear, so busy was she trying to come up with an ancestor while keeping Antonio from drinking too much espresso. "You might be onto something, Andrea. Give me a minute, and I will be right there."

I listened as well and used an enchantment to write those lines to my memory so I wouldn't forget them in the heat of battle.

Brian and Gloria were trying to settle Sheriff Buford's nerves. He was on the phone, worried we'd have an all-out war explode into the town from the prison depths. He was wondering how to keep the innocents safe. Gloria had the stellar idea of moving the entrance as far away from the town as possible but still kept it relevant. It was now sharing the parking lot with the Everlasting Love of The Lord Upon High Holy Redeemer Evangelical Church belonging to Oliver Brewster and his bitter wife, Laura.

The Brewster were the kind of folks that deserved a paranormal army to appear in their backyard. But we would protect even them.

Lorcan kept hugging me whenever he'd feel a spike in my energy—which usually meant I was about to go dark. "Stay with me, Tink. I know you want to go rushing to find her. But you need to wait until we can get some tactical defenses set up. I won't ask you to promise you will stay out of trouble or leave us to battle for you. I could never ask you to be less than what you were born to be. Just don't go all dark witch just yet."

I placed my hand on his face then gave him a soft kiss choosing not to respond. I couldn't.

"What is it?"

"I think I need to figure this out on my own, Lor."

"Oh, Tink. I was afraid you were going to say that. Here's the thing. I've been having these weird feelings, strange emotions coming out of nowhere. When I woke up this morning, I could swear I heard a voice say: everything is the opposite of what you will be told. Only I don't know what that means."

"Opposite? I have to think about that. But really, Lorcan. I need to go."

He hugged me even harder, if that was even possible, and whispered in my ear, "I love you."

My eyes opened wide, and my heart wanted to burst. I didn't answer Lorcan. Not yet.

Uncle Owen and Aunt Chiara had left to head to the Council. They had to deflect any rumors and keep them from just blowing up the prison instead. Not with the possibility of Adelaide being down there. They had enough clout, especially since Chiara was the Director.

Everyone else was arguing the best way to handle this raid.

Everyone but Grandpa Antonio. He chatted with Caliente

Saunders and kept sneaking more espresso, despite Adriana's efforts.

"Liliana. Vieni qua. You come-a speak to you grandpo."

I slipped away from Lorcan, raising a finger, so he knew I wanted him to wait a moment, then I gave him a gentle smile. I threw my arms open really wide and winked.

He looked puzzled but returned the smile.

Then I headed to where Antonio was sitting.

"Grandpa—*pa.*" I smiled at the old man. Or old witch, rather.

"Si. Is what I said. Grandpo."

I laughed, letting it go and let go of my nerves along with it.

Caliente moved her legs so I could get by and sit beside my great-grandfather. I couldn't get over how tall she was. She had to be a hair over six feet, and I knew there wasn't a runway around that wouldn't kill to have her strut her stuff on their catwalk.

Wicked was sitting with them and kept batting at Antonio's tie.

"What's up?" I asked.

"I was just having this fascinating conversation with Antonio. It seems he has recalled some lore about that ring laying on the floor over there. It passed down through Adriana's family from Roman times down to when Marcus stole it, then somehow remained unnoticed down to Adriana.

"Antonio remembers finding the ring one day and sensing the power in it. He chose to tuck it away so no one in the family would find it. So, he was the one to seal it in that silver box. Charles discovered it before Antonio could figure out where to hide it. He couldn't open it, so he brought it to Antonio, who told him the long history of it and warned him never to open it, never use it and keep it locked away."

I listened to her story then turned to my great-grandfather. "Did you ever tell grandmother that you had shown the box to Charlie?"

"Si. She is no happy he found out and she make give to Susie papa...he examines, and tell Cirino to put in cupboard. He say no open until you have-a book and ring. Have-a be together, ma no, you need to have, ok?"

So, Susanne Washington's father told my dad, Charlie, to stick the silver box in the cupboard in the forbidden library and hide the key separate but close. Susanne is now the Keeper of Tomes, like her father before her and his father before that. What did he mean by not opening it until you had the book and ring together? I had the ring. What book could he possibly be talking about?

Then a lightbulb went on. Susanne! *The wee book!*

"Excuse me a minute, please?" I stood up and rushed over to Susanne, sitting quietly beside Adriana. She was listening to everyone talk at once.

"Susanne, a minute, please?" I asked.

"Of course, sugar. What do you need?"

"Do you still have that tiny book in your purse? The one you were fussing over the other day when you were cleaning up your chamber?" I crossed my fingers that she hadn't chucked it in a pile somewhere.

"Why... yes, I do, love. Why do you need it?"

"I think I know what it is and what I'm supposed to do with it. Trust me to keep it for you awhile?"

"Of course, dear. Please keep it safe, though. I still need to find out all the details on it and record it down in my records."

"I promise. I will keep it as safe as I can."

Susanne removed the book from her purse and thanking her. I ran back over to Caliente and Antonio.

"I think this might be the book." I placed it in the palm of my hand and held it up so they both could see it.

Caliente recoiled away from my palm and wrinkled her nose. "I believe you are correct. This book holds some powerful dark magic. I can feel it pulsing."

We sat examining it as much as we could, what with Antonio's aged eyesight, my youthful eyes, and Caliente refusing to get close enough to see if she'd be able to read it. I even tried snapping a photo of the open book with my phone, but it would pixelate to the point of a blurry mess, so that was out. It wasn't until I heard a loud alarm go off and Edith popped in that help came when least expected, yet again.

I sat back, blinking at her, and opened my mouth.

Shooting her finger in my direction, she declared, "You are the one who wanted me to set off a bell or alarm before I popped in, so stuff it."

I clamped my mouth shut. Right behind Edith was Aunt Moira, once again rocking and knitting in her floating chair.

"I have great news for you, Lily. I got rid of Gordon for you. Poof! Gone!"

Groaning, I held my head in my hands and asked, "What did you do to him? Please don't tell me he is frozen in some kind of ghost hell of your making?"

Edith gave me a droll look and explained, "I told him we solved who killed him...that it was that shifter Geraldine creature. Once I did, his walkway appeared, and the Light showed up. Only the big idiot didn't want to move on. He still had a bone to pick with you, but I told him to give it up. I finally had to distract him with his heart's desire. A dude from the other side showed up with a Harley and dangled the keys in front of Gordon, who couldn't resist. So off he went on his moving sidewalk to the great beyond."

I was blinking again. My hand may have itched to pull out some hair as well, but I kept it together.

"Edith. Are you *seriously* telling me there is a moving sidewalk that brings you to The Light? Like, for real? And a Harley?"

"Yes. It came for me several times until I finally managed to evade it. Now I only catch glimpses of it here and there."

My heart began to ache, and I felt a mixture of pity and love for this distractible ghost of mine. "Edith, how many times have you let the light come and go?"

"I've lost count, I guess."

"But don't you think you should perhaps consider moving on?"

Big giant ghostly teardrops began slowly running down Edith's pale face. She didn't bother wiping them but instead blinked them away then answered me. "Lily. I'm a big help to you, aren't I? I mean, I warned you about that nasty perv. I helped you with the Forbidden Library. There is so much I can do for you if you'd just let me stay!"

"But what if you lose your chance to move on forever?" I worried, trying to get Edith to think long and hard about her predicament.

"What if I can't *move* on to a better place until I make up for all the bad stuff I've done, and helping you is one way I can do it?" She uttered softly. Looking up, I noticed Moira nodding her head yes, and decided it would be wise not to push Edith away for some time.

"Well then, Edith. Do you think you can manage to see what this little book has written in it? We've tried everything, to no avail! No matter what we've tried, the words are too small to see."

"That's because you are very big...but I can make myself positively tiny!" She cried. And she did just that. Swirling down to a minuscule Edith half the size of my pinky finger, she pretended to sit on my palm, but no matter what she did, she could grasp the book. "Some help, please?"

I propped the book open in front of her, and she began to

read. Then Edith began to laugh.

"What?"

"Oh, this book has a sense of humor. It says one line. *To grow big, just add water.*"

Oh, you had to be kidding me. I looked at Caliente, who was openly laughing... but Grandpa Antonio had fallen asleep.

"Can you excuse me a minute? Again?"

I ran upstairs and into my bathroom to get a small dropper and pulled in some water from my sink. Placing the book on my window seat, I used exactly one drop on the book and watched in amazement as it grew to standard size. Well, I say standard, but it was large, like a coffee table book, large.

It immediately began to whisper to me in a beautiful voice that purred in a flirty way. Definitely feminine.

"Hmm...this witch seems familiar. Do I know it? Yes! But not so formally, that I'd need a new dress. I know its parents, girl of red, black-haired boy, such hidden talents, they gave me joy. Adelaide and Charlie, sitting in a tree...look what they've done now... it's their Sweet baby!"

"My name is Lily Sweet, yes. I am Adelaide and Charlie's daughter. You are correct." I fumbled my words, amazed that a book was sentient.

"Sentient, yes. And I read minds too. What is it you wish of me little Lily, daughter of two? Dark witches both, and favorite of mine...always were fun, and they taught me to rhyme!"

Adelaide and Charlie taught the book to rhyme? Really?

"Do you know what I need to do to defeat the shifter that I'm searching for? She told my mother you belonged to her, but she shrunk you down then lost you. Are you loyal to her, or will you help me, instead?"

"Shrank, stank, blank book I see. Not loyal to one who

would do such to me! The one you speak of did not own me, no. It's the other way around. I created her so!"

"You created her? But... how?" I pulled the hefty tome onto my lap and sat cross-legged on my bed.

"She found me one day, asked me to make her immortal. I sent her to a vampire who lived through a portal. He turned her with blood, but she staked him with wood, she became what she sought, but her heart is no good."

Her heart is no good. No good. She's evil. I think that's what the book meant!

"How can I defeat her? She is trying to open wards to our witch prison. A bad witch named Donna Fredricks created an army of very evil creatures down there. This shifter wants to free them into the world. I think she also took Adelaide... my mother. Adelaide put on a ruby ring that belongs to my great-grandmother's family. The Romano coven. When Adelaide put the ring on, she faded away, and the ring remained behind. Please, can you help?"

"Hmmm. Hmmm, yes. The ring is foul to those who are wrong, but for the heir apparent, it makes one strong. Donna and Deanna, evil are they. Made a nasty bargain with a witch one day. The witch was a shifter and told them lies. Then she became a changeling, now everyone dies!"

No. I refused to believe everyone would die. I wouldn't let it happen. I would embrace my darkness and fight this evil even if it left me no better, bringing me down to their level.

"Really? Would you turn dark to save every creature you love? Would you give up your soul never go up above? Could you do this little witch siren? Could you do this for me? Or would you rather save one who is bound by the tree?"

Bound by the tree. Tree? Trees are made out of wood. Wait! "Do you mean, instead of having to turn evil to beat the shifter in a fight, all I need to do is promise to free the vampire that betrayed who is impaled somewhere?"

"Indeed, you are right...the vampire won't end. He's stuck in a grave, and I mourn for my friend. Betrayal by this witch has cost her times three. Win against her you shall if you do this for me!"

"I promise you I will save your vampire friend. Tell me where he is bound, and I will remove the wooden stake and free him. Just tell me how to defeat the shifter."

"When death takes hold, a change will come. That's when you stand strong...don't think to run! It's what you need; it's all you seek. When silver meets undead, that's when she is weak. It's all in the eyes; she will fool you, you see. Don't believe all she offers, especially her plea. Instead, use your darts and aim for her eyes. You'll save her with truth, but kill her with lies."

And I was doing so well up to this point. What does she mean I will save her with truth but kill her with lies?

"Wait! Who will I save with the truth? Who will I kill with lies? Do you mean two different people, or are we talking about the same person... the shifter?"

"Wise is the witchling. She uncovers the truth. The shifter has one name, and it isn't Ruth. Study your lineage and find who you seek, but don't spend all day there. Just take one small peek. When you have your name set, and you don the ring, never once use the truth, it isn't your thing! Go for the trickster, tell only lies. If you fail this one task, dear...*your mother will die.*"

My blood ran cold, and the weight of everything I had to remember was starting to make me doubt I could do this and succeed. I was about to take the book down to Caliente, or Adriana, anyone—and pray they could figure out what it meant. But somehow, I knew I needed to be the one to fight this battle. And do it without anyone's help. I had to be strong.

"I think I'm ready. But I need to know where your

vampire friend is. And I need to know where I can take a peek at my lineage."

Suddenly the book began to flip its pages, faster and faster until it stopped on a page toward the back. It was a genealogy with illustrations! I quickly scanned the page and saw my name with a tiny drawing of me! Going up from there, I rushed through the rest. Charlie, Adriana, Luigi, Marcus...until I landed on the female witch whose ring I needed to put on. Lucretia Romano. She was illustrated there with her hand across her heart. On her hand was the ring. I had her name. I memorized her face. She wouldn't be able to trick me with deception now that I knew what she looked like!

Bam!

The book slammed shut, and it began to hum quietly to itself but not before whispering, "At the end of it all, desperation and lies, say her name despite doubt, and the old witch dies! The reverse is her lie, you know. Do what I say so Red can throw. Oh...and she really hates cats."

What the heck? Some of it made sense.

"At the end of it all. Got it. But red and throw? What about the vampire? Your friend. Where is he? And cats? That end doesn't even rhyme!"

The book didn't respond.

"Am I to bring you downstairs...or will you stay here safe in my room?"

The book stopped humming and became very ordinary looking, then shrunk back down to the size of a cracker.

"Ok, then. Here you will remain, safe on my bed. I promise I will free your vampire friend if and when I find him."

Waiting for another few ticks to see if the book would say anything else, I sat down on my bed to consider my next move. I had Lucretia's name and now a face to go with it. I decided, of the two witches in Adelaide's story, this one being the old hag who tied Charlie's life to the rose bush and pretended to be Geraldine, had me pleased to be the one to take her out. Would I have the chance to find the one who was the coven leader? Did it matter anymore? After all, no coven ever showed up. So maybe that was an elaborate ruse. I couldn't keep it straight and feared that thinking too hard would distract me from what I needed to do right now!

I quickly changed into a snug black mock turtleneck and tight leggings and put on my boots with good traction. I made sure my sweetbriar earring, necklace, and ring were secured on me and headed back downstairs.

Everyone was still arguing and making plans.

I walked over to Caliente, who had relocated to the den, and sat across from the ring. It was still on the floor where it had dropped.

I leaned forward and whispered, "I think you know what I am about to do."

Caliente smiled. Her blood-red lips were parting to show off brilliant white teeth and just ever so slightly protruding fangs. "I think you are about to put on that ring and go fight your own battle."

"Got it in one."

We stared at one another for a few more minutes, then I asked, "Do you know of a vampire who is impaled some-where by a piece of wood? Aware but frozen, unable to free himself?"

Caliente looked shocked, then grief-stricken with anger. "I do. I know of one who has been gone for many years now. But rumor has it that he was betrayed by a witch and frozen by wood...right through his heart. Or what we have as a heart, anyway."

"Do you know where he is? Any clue?"

Caliente regarded me for longer than I felt comfortable,

although I didn't break the silence. "You will find him wherever that ring takes you, I would think. The last anyone saw of him; he was purported to be helping the witch who put that curse on this trinket here. The next thing we knew, they both vanished. Find the witch, and you will find the vampire."

"You know this will take me to the lower level of the prison. My family will try to follow me by heading to the main entrance. I hope to wrap this up before any creatures are released, and any of my family members arrive to save the day. Think you can stall them for me?"

"I can try." She agreed. And that's all I could hope for.

I stood up and gave everyone I loved one final look. I knew I would have hurt feelings and anger to deal with. I just hoped they would understand I needed to do this alone. Somehow, I knew this was the way it was supposed to go down. I just hoped I lived to hear the scolding I'd receive when I came back. When. When I came back.

I smiled and whispered, "Here I come, mom." Then I reached down to pick up the ring. Before I could place it on my finger, Lorcan saw what I was about to do and shouted. Then the room fell silent for just a few seconds until an enormous outcry rang out. I slowly slipped the ring on my finger just as Wicked flew through the air and landed on my shoulders. Then everything began to fade.

Lorcan ran to me, but Caliente held him back, and I whispered the words, "I don't love you."

Lorcan's eyes widened in shock and confusion for just a moment, and then he smiled with sadness and understanding.

Then I was no more.

CHAPTER 19

I seriously no longer existed for the count of ten. I had no arms, legs, or head. I couldn't move, couldn't feel... couldn't see. None of my senses worked, and I felt like I was drifting—floating. I was flotsam in a room of emptiness. Suddenly, I had the sensation I was falling, but all I did was open my eyes. I found myself in a stone chamber with a cobblestone floor and flickering sconces on the wall. The room was round, and there were six arches with hallways leading down each to places unknown.

I took the one in front of me, instinctively knowing it was the correct one. When I reached the end, I found another chamber. This one larger, with only one way in and another way out. In the middle of the room was a table and two chairs. On the table was a tiny wooden box and two goblets. Sitting in one of the chairs was a slight blonde woman, unremarkable in appearance. She glanced my way but then went back to her task.

She was reading a paperback book, and when I drew near, I was surprised to see it was a romance novel by an unknown author, to me anyway. Next to her, on the corner of the table, was a button, red and straightforward in design. It looked like all you could do to it was push down on it. Beside it was a remote intercom.

Ok then.

I settled my nerves and subtly called up enough dark magic to remain calm, therefore not allowing her a glimpse at my thoughts. I sat in the chair across from her and waited until she spoke. This took some time because she seemed engrossed in her book. I guessed about fifteen minutes went by, then she suddenly sighed, like the weight of the world was upon her.

"Are you here to ask questions?" Her voice was high and prissy sounding and grated. I wanted to call her Karen.

I remembered I must always lie, and even though I had a million of them, I replied, "No."

"Liar!" The woman pressed the button and spoke into the intercom, "You may kill prisoner number one."

I jumped a bit as someone began screaming in pain. This went on for a minute until his voice was cut off and slowly faded into a gurgling quiet. I felt queasy and kept swallowing down my nausea. I kept telling myself not to be tricked by deceit and roll with this, whatever this was! I smiled.

"Pity." She picked up her book, but I could tell she wasn't reading this time. I waited another five minutes, and again, she spoke.

"Would you like to see what is in this box?"

Again. The obvious answer would be for me to say yes. I had a feeling, despite its size, a vampire would in there with a wooden stake in his heart.

"Not really."

"Liar!" Again, pushing the button, the woman spoke into the intercom and said, "You may kill prisoner number two."

The screaming came from a female voice this time, and I would almost swear it sounded like Andrea. I began to sweat, but still, I pretended boredom was my only mien—center myself, breath in, breath out. Calm.

"You do want to see what's in this box, don't you? And I know I'm right because you like to solve mysteries, right?"

"Not really." I yawned and laid my head down across my arms pretending to try and sleep.

"Liar!" Again, the button and intercom. "You may kill prisoners three and four and make sure they suffer."

This time I heard two people, I think they were women again, shrieking in pain and begging for mercy. This went on for longer than I thought I could take, but then silence reigned, and I began to examine my nails.

"Do you want to see your mother?"

"I have no mother." That was a lie, and I was curious to see what she'd say in reply. Great. Now I'm rhyming.

"Of course, you have a mother! Everyone has a mother! Now, do you want to see your mother or not?"

"I don't have a mother. Sorry." Not sorry. That was an easy lie.

"Liar! Young lady. Do you, or do you not have a mother? You must give me an answer for us to proceed!"

"I don't have a mother." Right then, I knew the answer I was to give to move beyond this point. "I don't have a mother... I have two."

The room got dark except for the box on the table and two windows opening in the walls. In one was my mother, Adelaide. Alert and observing me. In the other, my Aunt Jessica, who seemed to be sleeping standing up, was dressed in the simple white sleeping gown she always wore. I still had one of her old nightgowns, but I hardly wore it because it would be covered in black fur if I did.

Black fur!

Where was Wicked? Did she remain behind? Did she come on this side, or is she lost forever? I began to tremble but knew I needed to get my act together and not let this get me rattled, or I'd never get my mother back.

I turned when I heard a noise behind me and saw a chair gliding toward me that stopped just before it touched my legs.

"You may sit down." A different voice this time.

I so no reason not to, so I sat.

The room began to turn, but I remained still. The table was now behind me, but in front of me was a six-sided coffin. Full-sized. Easily long enough to hold someone who touched seven feet tall. Chester and Hester would be thrilled.

A woman appeared next to the coffin and began fiddling with the locks. She had black hair, like mine, and was remarkable in appearance...her eyes were lilac. When she glanced at me, I knew I was looking at Lucretia. When she managed to break the locks open, she swung the door wide, and I beheld a male vampire, frozen. Eyes open and alive, but utterly paralyzed. The only thing he managed to move was his eyes, so he stared into mine. A wooden stake was in his heart.

"Do you believe in love at first sight? I wonder. The heart is a fragile thing. If you answer this wrong, I will have no choice but to set this monster free, and he will grab you then bite you so he can drink. He is hungry. Very, very hungry." Her voice was less grating, but it still made me want to slap her.

I turned to look at the woman, all smug and superior and wanted to knock her down a few pegs.

"You have a lover. Lorcan, I believe his name is. Look at this undead creature impaled through the heart. It must hurt something awful—heartache and despair, so lovely. If you break Lorcan's heart, he will be in such pain. You must love him so. Has he told you he loved you yet? I wonder. If he has told you those words, what was your reply?"

The look she gave me was filled with anticipation; her excitement was palpable.

I smiled and replied. "I told Lorcan, 'I don't love you!'"

"Liar!" She shrieked and tore at her eyes, spinning in frustration and pacing away from me. I didn't hesitate but jumped up and pulled the stake out of the vampire's heart.

"You fool! He will kill you. He is evil! He hates everything, and he needs to feed. What? No!" The woman wailed when instead of grabbing me, the vampire lunged at the evil witch, crushing her body to his. Fangs extended, and arms locked around her torso like a vice, he snarled.

"Wait! Stop! Please. Please don't harm me. Look...look around you. Don't you see them? Look at what lies beyond this room."

The chamber lit up, and the wall on one side where Adelaide and Jessica stood remained the same, but the wall on the opposite side became transparent and filmy. The air seemed to wave and quiver, and when I looked beyond, I saw someone who caused my blood to freeze to ice. Donna Fredricks was standing there with a hoard of demonic creatures. Witches, trolls, a few giants, vampires, and many more whose Breed I could not identify. I knew the wards were about to come down unless I could best the despicable witch.

I looked down when I realized she was staring at my hand...at the ruby ring.

"Do you like this? Is this yours?" I asked her.

"I don't answer you. You answer me!"

"I don't think you can win against the vampire." That was the truth. I thought she might best him unless we both took her on as a team effort.

"I win! I win! You know he is stronger than me. I'm just a witch! You lied...you lied!"

I pulled out my silver darts and looked right at the

massive immortal, and screamed, "I need you to stand right there and not move an inch!"

The vampire nodded slightly and immediately ducked. Luckily, he seemed to understand the lie, to tell the truth, thing I had going on.

I began to rapid-fire the darts at the witch, aiming for her eyes, and managed to get several in them while she howled in pain before she turned her head. Immediately she shifted, and I saw an old woman, ancient yet regal looking, like a Roman goddess that suddenly became mortal and aged. She was the older version of the illusion she put up—such vanity.

I quickly flicked my eyes around the room but could no longer see the vampire.

The witch took a deep breath and seemed amazed she could breathe at all. I hit her with more darts, and she cried out to me. "Stop! Wait! I can help you! I can bring them back. Your mother. Both of them. I can bring them back, but I will take them both with me if you kill me. I've bound them in blood. Their souls are mine."

Before I could respond, the witch lashed out with magic that slammed into me, throwing me back and causing me to drop the darts. I reached out and sent a stream of dark magic pouring out of me but couldn't see what I was doing. The pain had temporarily blinded me.

Before I could stand, the witch was on me and began to shift into people I knew, Geraldine, Barbara, even old Mrs. Riley from where I'd last lived in New York. Then she turned into Brian and bared her fangs, sinking them into my neck.

I screamed. The pain coursing through me was dark. Black and vile. I immediately wanted to hurl. My hand slowly crept out as I felt in the darkness for the pouch holding the silver darts. Instead, I found one lone dart on the floor near me. Despite my better judgment, I raised my hand and plunged the silver missile directly into my eye.

Instead of feeling pain, I felt hope.

The witch screeched and shifted once more. I was looking at my father, Charlie. Then I was slammed backward with such force I thought I might have broken my back. Shackles appeared, binding me to the floor, which rose suddenly, and I tilted upward, facing my mother and aunt.

"She will die. Your mother will die."

I was astounded when I saw both Adelaide and Jessica turn to me, both looking well and staring at me. I remembered what the book said. As long as I didn't use magic and picked the silver up, I would have an unlimited supply.

Moving my hand, I could tell I held one, but with my hands shackled, what choice did I have? I needed to use magic to break free.

"I have the book with me."

"Now you lie. How dare you lie!" I screamed in agony as she hurled spikes at me, impaling me to the board when they slid into my body and came out the other side of me.

"I'm not lying," I gasped. "I have the book with me."

"Impossible. It's a book. It's big, and it whispers and talks. You couldn't possibly have it."

"I have the book with me. It is massive! It is the size of my pinky nail." All lies...as it was safely at home and the size was more like a Cheez-It cracker!

I saw the witches' eyes light up as she remembered the book had been shrunk by Jessica, as promised.

"My mother shrunk the book."

"There you go! See? See how easy it was, to tell the truth?"

I began to cough, and blood bubbled up and out of my mouth. I thought I might be close to dying and wondered if I was mistaken. It was getting harder to breathe, and the pain was going to cause me to black out.

"There, there, Lily Sweet. I won. I won—you poor baby.

You want to rest now, don't you? You want to run to your mommy and have her hold you."

I felt the shackles slide off me and I was no longer impaled, yet the pain remained excruciating as I stumbled but managed to stay on my feet.

"You have one chance to say goodbye. You lost, Lily Sweet, so they both will die at my hands, as will you, ending the line I despised. No more Dolce to Sweet. You are the last. Hurry up! Go to your mother, and don't even think of trying to use your magic on me. I have double the strength over you. Both of my parents were dark witches!"

I began a painful trek across the floor, paused in the center, and looked at Jessica. I didn't know if she was standing behind that window by some magic, but I raised my hand and blew her a kiss with the thought, I love you. Then sent the kiss in her direction and crossed the floor to Adelaide's window. Just before I reached her, I saw Jessica move, so I paused. She returned my air kiss with one of her own and mouthed, "I love you," coming back to me as her reply. I felt strength in my spirit even though my body seemed damaged beyond repair.

I reached Adelaide and turned to face the witch, who cackled with glee.

"You fool! Can't you see straight, dearie? You're standing in front of Adelaide! Ha, ha, ha...you foolish, foolish child. I might have taken pity on you and let one of them go. But now your mistake has cost you everything."

My head had been hanging low, waiting for my magic to coil up. I knew I needed to land a direct hit on the old hag's eyes before I could let my dark magic out, but I also knew I needed to get as many in there as I could. I readied my hands, feeling the darts multiply, then looked directly at the witch.

My eyes were black.

"What trickery is this? What are you? Why are your eyes

blackened like that?" With her eyes wide open in fear, I flung my arms forward and willed the silver darts to fly true, smiling in satisfaction when several of the missiles landed in both of the witch's eyes.

It was her turn to wail, and I was thrilled to see the vampire back and once again locking her in his iron embrace. The hag began to shift over and over, and each time she did, the vampire would tear at her. Unable to remain in one shape for long, the vampire began to wrest her essence away from her body with the intent to split her in two, effectively removing her vampirism and leaving nothing but a shadow of the shifter she once was.

"Wait! *Stop!* The wards will come down whether or not you best me. And your mother and aunt will still die. The only way to stop this is to answer one more question. Who are your parents?"

I was shocked. All this time, I assumed the last question she would ask was for me to say her name. Now, what would I do? I couldn't believe this. If I blew this chance to take out the vilest witch to attack my family, everything Jessica sacrificed, every long year Adelaide lost stuck inside Wicked, all the horrors my dad, Charlie, might have faced... might still be suffering; all of it would be for nothing.

As I wracked my brain trying to come up with the correct answer, I saw movement behind the vampire. It was small and dark, and I couldn't quite make out what it was. That is until I heard a cry of alarm from the old witch as she tried to hop and wrestle the vampire at the same time.

"Eek, what is that...fur...is it a cat? Get it off me! Get it away. It will take my soul if she says my name! Get it away. Just answer the question...do it...who are your parents?" Fear and loathing met panic, but nothing could release the hold the vampire had on the witch. So, she finally stopped thrashing but mewed a bit in agony.

"Who are your parents?" she shouted one last time.

Wicked walked out from between her ankles and trotted over to me as I let all my dark magic come up and out. I smiled at the monstrous woman and replied.

"My parents are Charles Sweet and Adelaide Croy..."

I saw her eyes fill with visions of victory, even as this bit of news shocked her... that is until I completed my answer.

"...*Lucretia.*"

The entire room began to swirl, and I could feel the wall behind me crumble. I sensed my mother before I felt the rush of air pass me as she threw her dagger at the old hag. Just as the blade hit its mark, the vampire ripped the last of Lucretia's soul, letting the body drop to the floor. It began to blacken and rot.

Adelaide came to stand by me, and together we watched as the veil that separated our area from the prison began to stitch itself closed. Donna started to pound her fists on the barrier, but the wards held. The look she gave us was one of such hatred, I knew she'd not rest until we were all dead.

That's OK. I felt the same about her and that army she created. I even gave her a one-finger salute as the veil became solid and unyielding. Donna howled.

I could see the vampire holding the essence of the old witch...my fourth great-grandmother—and watched with emotions a bit detached as her body on the floor turned to dust. Even in this shifter form of swirling inky goo, I knew she would never be anything but ether. Hitting her eyes with so many darts prevented her from being able to see where to shift, trapping her 'in-between.'

The vampire released the last vestige of Lucretia, and she dissolved into mist and was no more.

"Mreow!" said Wicked.

"Indeed," Adelaide replied.

Turning, I became alarmed when I saw Jessica

gone...those walls also solid. That is until the ancient vampire began to speak.

"She was never really there, Lily Sweet. It was an illusion. Even as Lucretia Dolce is but a wisp of black smoke, destined to roam the corridors as nothing more than a shattered spirit, so too is her magic.

"That wasn't my Aunt Jessica?"

"She was an illusion, my dear. But do not let this trouble you. For I believe she was watching over you, and the love was here with you, nevertheless. She heard your love to her, and she returned it...you felt it, I'm sure."

"I believe I did."

The vampire smiled, which made me want to take a step back. Someone should tell these guys it might be better if they came up with a new way to show happiness.

"Oh, and I thank you for my release."

"You're welcome. I think I'm about to pass out."

Adelaide placed her arm around my shoulder in case I should fall. "Steady, love. I'm here."

I leaned into her, grateful but weak.

"I will heal you before you cross over." I looked wide-eyed at the vampire, and he smiled and hurriedly explained what he meant. "Cross back... to your home. And no, I am also a healer, not just a vampire. I will not turn you into one of us."

Adelaide released her hold on me as the vampire placed his hand on my forehead and frowned. My mother bent down to retrieve her dagger, and I was surprised to see it didn't have a mark on it. She tucked it back into her boot and said, "I'm rather glad you didn't take it from me, all things considered."

Yeah... good call, that.

I turned to the vampire as I felt myself heal and felt nothing but wonder as my body renewed. "Thank you, that was incredible. Oh...what's your name? I'm sorry, I should have asked."

"That is fine. You have had a bit going on to remember such niceties. I am Valgaard."

"It's a pleasure to meet you Valgaard. The book will be happy to know you are free."

"Ah! My old friend. Tell her I said I might see her again, someday. Right now, though, it is time for you to leave. Oh... and you may keep the ring, it is cursed no more." He announced with his somber voice starting to fade as I felt myself drifting and floating again.

"Wait. What about my mother? And my cat?"

"Will be with you as well. Close your eyes, my dear. And tell my daughter I said, 'I love you.'"

"Your..." He must mean Caliente!

But I never got to finish what I was asking the vampire because I suddenly found myself surrounded by everyone I loved.

I did it.

CHAPTER 20

*"W*ake up, Birthday Girl! Happy Birthday, darling!"

"Mommy, mommy! I want cake! Can I have my cake now? Can I?"

"Lily! You have an entire day ahead of you. Let's enjoy it, and you can have cake later this evening, after your Birthday dinner."

"But I want cake now! Daddy! Daddy! Can I have my cake now...right now?"

"Why, Lily? Why can't you wait like a good girl and have your cake when everyone else does after your dinner tonight?"

"Because, Mommy, because, Daddy. I'm not a good girl! I'm a *dark* witch!"

"Well then, I guess it's time for some cake!"

"Yay! Cake, for breakfast, is good."

* * *

"Wake up, Birthday Girl. Happy Birthday!"

I opened my eyes, blinking away the memory that haunted my dreams. I could feel the sand still in my eyes and began rubbing them, then looked around my room.

That's when I saw Adelaide, my mother, standing in the doorway, holding a Birthday cake that I assumed came from my Uncle Stephen's café. I looked up and met her eyes, damp with tears, and felt mine get misty as well.

"Who wants a big piece of Birthday cake right now?" Adelaide asked.

"Just one piece? That's no fun...I'm a *dark* witch!"

* * *

LATER THAT DAY, as the March winds blew and the chill in the air gave way to a promise of springtime weather, I found myself surrounded by all my family and friends and people who I thought might be family—just don't ask me their names!

The Italian side dominant and loud, telling stories and drinking wine. The Scottish delegation present and accounted for, drinking whisky and equally noisy.

Lorcan was sitting on my right and Adelaide on my left.

Andrea, Jake, Becky, Brian, Martha, Keisha, and Steve Junior were having a rousing game of who can catch an olive when you toss it in the air? Even cousin Douglas looked mildly interested.

Edith was singing Scottish folk songs with Moira...of course, there weren't many people in the room who could hear them. Lucky me.

My dining room table was stretched open, and a few card tables had been added on either end, draped with plastic lace tablecloths and just enough chairs, so everyone had a seat.

Aunt Chiara went all out and made several trays of lasagna, and Grandpa Antonio broke out his homemade grappa. He was currently dancing the polka in the living room with Adriana, the love of his life. He looked a gnomish version of Alastair Sims from the old movie, A Christmas Carol, the way he was lifting his leg high and whirling my great-grandmother around the room. Most of my cousins were clapping along to their antics.

Bowls of antipasto and platters of cold cuts were passing around with several different choices for dinner rolls. I couldn't count all the items. Olives and cheese. Squid and shrimp cocktail. Soppressata and pepperoni. Grapes and raspberries...and figs, dried and fresh.

There was a prime rib roast in the oven with potatoes and a salad in the wings. I didn't know where we'd stuff it all, but the men dedicated themselves to the task.

I was on my third Whisky Sour and felt no pain.

Mortimer and Caliente even tried one each, but I knew they'd pay for it later on when their bodies rejected it. They were good eggs for trying. I'm sure Adriana would crack open a keg of blood for them soon. Caliente admitted to me that Valgaard was her father and thanked me for helping free him and giving her his message.

No. We didn't storm the prison to kill Donna and her minions. That was coming. And no, we hadn't tried to combine Adelaide's hair with Charlie's and make a new potion to strengthen the spell and try and bring my dad home. That was coming as well.

There were so many horrible things coming down the pike. It made my head dizzy with the possibilities...but today, I wasn't going to let that ruin my day.

This was my very first birthday party at home. I take that back. This was my very first birthday party in my home *since* I've come back to Sweet Briar. To tell you the truth, I kind of forgot about it because Jessica, my dear aunt, never celebrated hers or mine. It's not like we could have afforded the cake anyway. But I didn't mind. I knew she loved me beyond reason. I even walked to her grave this morning and left her a slice of my breakfast birthday cake...complete with a lit candle and a plastic fork. I swear I felt her hug me.

This doesn't mean there isn't another cake waiting for dinner to be over, then presents and the big reveal with twenty-six candles ringing in a new year—for me, anyway.

We hadn't yet sat down to discuss the why. Why Lucretia Dolce went down this dark path, prolonging her life and becoming a vampire with the sole intent to destroy all her direct heirs...after having a bit of fun with them. I'm sure we'd figure it all out... or not. I'm not sure I cared.

We'd deal with Donna.

We'd get to the mysterious coven leader.

My family would take on the rogue Romano coven in the Pacific Northwest.

I would bring my dad back home and give him and Adelaide a chance to be a couple...and enjoy their marriage.

Look at Adriana and Antonio, now sitting on the sofa and laughing, surrounded by their tribe. That is what my parents deserved.

Nothing these evil asshats could throw at us would stop the love surrounding us this day...or any day. They could plot and scheme and try for world domination, but it doesn't matter.

Not really.

They will never win. Not when evil puts so much effort into obtaining power and prestige over what truly matters. Family. Good friends. Love. Being together and breaking bread and sharing laughter. That is what is real. That is why, no matter what life throws at us, we will always persevere.

Speaking of love.

The room grew quiet, and I woke from my reverie to see every single one of my guests staring at me.

Alrighty then. I know it's my Birthday and all... but what gives?

I heard the chair next to me scrape back as Lorcan stood up and removed something from his pocket. Imagine my surprise when he went down on one knee and opened a little velvet box that held the most exquisite aquamarine surrounded by diamonds.

What? Hang on a minute.

I'm going to kill him.

Oh... I will kiss him too. But right now? Yeah. He's dead to me.

"Lily. Right now, if I had to guess what you are thinking, I'd be fearing for my life."

Everyone chuckled, and I nodded yes, to let the big lug know he was definitely in trouble.

"I've loved you forever, and I spent weeks trying to come up with the perfect way to ask you the question I'm about to ask you. Nothing could come close to doing it like this...and by the way, the pressure to get this right is incredible..."

More laughter.

"I wanted to give you this memory to cherish forever, having everyone you love surrounding you at this moment. Anyway. I hope you aren't that upset with me. Lily Sweet. I love you. Will you be my wife?"

A million trite responses flitted through my mind, but in the end, I found myself nodding my head yes, and whispering loud enough for the room to hear my reply, "I never really wanted to be the ninja. I would love to be your princess, Lorcan. Yes... oh yes!"

Lorcan placed the box on the table and removed the ring, slipping it on my awaiting finger. Everyone cheered, and champagne corks popped. Then Wicked jumped on Lorcan's vacated seat and knocked the velvet box off the table and onto the floor in one swipe. That really set everyone off laughing.

"Meorw!"

After a few toasts and an embarrassing glass-rim-tapping frenzy that wouldn't stop until Lorcan and I kissed, I had a moment to show my mother the gorgeous stone Lorcan chose for my engagement ring.

Adelaide was oohing and aahing with June by her side. "You are going to make the most beautiful bride, my darling." She gushed.

I turned to find Lorcan gazing at me, and I leaned forward to touch my forehead to his. "I am going to kill you, you know."

"I know."

"And just for the record. I really don't love you."

Lorcan smiled. "I know that too. You *reeeeaally* love me."

"You got that right, Mister!"

Turning back to June, who had just asked me if we knew when we'd like to make it official and set a date, I answered with a laugh, "That is going to take some discussion when there isn't a plethora of relatives around to give their opinions!"

A few more chuckles until...

"Well... iffin' I had to guess. I'd say this means you kids ain't gonna have that there ménage à trois thingy I heard you were thinking of having."

"Abner!"

* * *

THANK YOU FOR READING! I hope you loved meeting Lily and Lorcan, and the rest of the characters. The next book in the Lily Sweet Mysteries is Witch and Peace. Will it be a happily ever after affair for Lily and Lorcan or will the danger that lies ahead get in the way of their happiness? Will Lily ever face Donna and get answers? Who is behind all of this? Will we ever find out?

CLICK HERE TO READ WITCH AND PEACE NOW >

And if you enjoyed Revenge is Sweet, Witch, you'll love Maggie and her quirky, sometimes funny, sometimes dark, but always magical paranormal gang of monster-hunting antique appraisers. A Tale of Two Sisters, the tie-in series to my Lily Sweet World, highlights Lily's cousins Maggie and Ellie Fortune and is FREE on Kindle Unlimited!

"I am loving the snark in this book."

- S. Keller, BookBub author reviews.

I appreciate your help in spreading the word, including telling friends and family. Reviews help readers find books! Please leave a review on your favorite book site.

You can also join my Facebook Group: Author Bettina M. Johnson's Team Wicked for exclusive giveaways and sneak peek of future books—and just plain silliness!

SIGN UP FOR BETTINA M. JOHNSON'S NEWS-LETTER: http://eepurl.com/gZKo51

Continue on for a short excerpt from Witch and Peace....

Witch and Peace

I SLOWLY TURNED over on the beach towel, stretching my arms above my head then tucking them behind my neck, luxuriating in the warm breeze as it gently caressed my body —the smell of the surf tickling my senses.

Rolling over onto my side, I traced one hand over the surface of the sand, each grain a gentle abrasive marvel on my fingertips as my eyes tracked Lorcan's approach. He rose out of the surf, his body glistening as the sun's rays made the droplets on his torso sparkle. He slowly made his way toward me with a seductive stride making my heartrate hitch in anticipation.

Dropping to his knees in front of me, he leaned forward as beads of water cascaded down his chest. His gaze bore into mine, warm and gentle yet hinting of wild things to come, as he smiled and brought his lips mere inches from my own. His sweet breath was a heady mixture of bacon and coffee, and I knew his kiss would render me...

Bacon?

Coffee?

My brain slammed on the brakes, pulling me slowly out of my reverie, rendering me fully awake. I was ensconced in my bed, sans beach towel, but wrapped in my blanket. There was nary a grain of sand in sight unless I counted the grimy bits set in the corners of my eyes. I began rubbing to chase away the last of what would undoubtedly have been one heck of a sweet dream. Taking stock of my situation, I concluded that the smells emanating from downstairs were most assuredly that of bacon and coffee, and I may even detect eggs to boot.

I sat up and peered around the room, looking for my cat, Wicked. She was nowhere around, but my open door gave me a hint of her whereabouts.

Glancing at the window, I noted it was still fairly dark outside, so I tracked my eyes over to my alarm clock. Six a.m.? Really?

It took me less than ten minutes to make a bathroom pit stop, don some slippers, and wander downstairs, where I heard the distinctive sound of human conversation. Considering I lived alone with my mother, Adelaide, as my roommate—and this a recent occurrence, I began to ponder just to whom she was conversing. That I had two ghosts popping in and out of my life made me consider it might be they with whom mom was having her lively discourse.

Shuffling along, I made my way to the kitchen and came to an abrupt halt.

Adelaide was, indeed, chatting away, but it was Lorcan she was speaking to—he, the man in my dreams, until I remember he'd proposed and was, in fact, my fiancé. I still am not processing this. Wicked was sitting on the counter watching Lorcan flip eggs while Adelaide was draining the bacon, carefully straining the liquid fat into a lard jar while trapping the bits in a strainer as any proper southern lady would. What had me agog—or who, rather—was sitting at my kitchen table, in my spot, eating a heaping plate of pancakes, drinking the aforementioned coffee—and using my mug!

"Nempf!" I think that was the sound that came out of me, anyway.

"Lily! Darling. Good morning," Adelaide said, smiling at me as she placed the tray of bacon back in the oven. We must be feeding an army because another plate of bacon was ready for consumption on the counter.

"Hey, baby." This from Lorcan, who expertly cracked another two eggs in the heavily-buttered pan.

I remained rooted to the floor.

"What's wrong, love?" Adelaide noticed my mien and became mildly concerned since I still had my mouth hanging open and couldn't form any coherent words.

I thrust my arm out—elbow locked, palm facing up with fingers tight, the thumb cocked and pointing in the direction of my chair.

"Nmeh."

"That's Abner, dear." She replied.

My brows went down into a deep V, and I manage to speak appropriately.

"I know that's Abner. But what is he doing here, and why is he in my spot?"

Abner paused from shoveling pancakes in his pie hole faster than a train conductor stoking the burner on a coal train. He responded with yet another utterance that would make Captain Obvious proud. "I'm eatin' break-fast."

Yes. Abner actually said break then fast.

"Why are you eating it here, again?"

"Gotta get them seedlings in the ground now that we are full on the spring planting season. Time is money." Abner replied.

Seedlings? Spring?

I looked out the window to see if anything had changed since I last made a note of the weather conditions. Yesterday evening, before I crept upstairs to bed, my life seemed as ordinary as my life could be with the assurances that we were in the middle of a late March ice storm. I was secure in the knowledge that not much had altered. The entire landscape looked like Jack Frost did a jig with Queen Elsa making the landscape safe for the residents of Arendelle. In other words:

"There are icicles everywhere, and the ground looks like permafrost."

In that instant, another strong gust rattled my windows as ice plinked against the panes. Even the fireplace sizzled as errant moisture reached the flames, emphasizing my point. So much for the shift in weather around my birthday earlier in the month, with its promise of spring!

That's the thing with the weather in the north Georgia mountains—things could change from year to year. One March, you could have cookouts and plant flowers while you put away your winter clothing, while the following year would find yourself huddled around your fireplace dreaming of global warming. This year was one for the record books as far as snow and cold were concerned.

"That's why I'm in here. No sense in planting when the ground's still a frozen like."

I slowly blinked as my face went blank. It took me a few minutes to process the fact that Abner had just told me he was here to plant. You know what? Yeah. I needed to stop thinking because I could feel my brain cells melting, never to regenerate again.

"Abner has seedlings ready for your greenhouse, Lily," Adelaide explained. "Then when this cold weather finally snaps, he can move them to your planting bed."

"Whatever happened to my peas? Are they dead?" I asked, remembering the little green nubs we added to the soil back in February when Donald Murphy, my friend, and an avid gardener, insisted they needed to be interred to the ground lest we miss their planting schedule.

Hold up. Was my greenhouse usable?

"No. Peas know when to come up. They will jest wait for a spell until the soil tells them it's time. Then there's no holding them back. Don't you worry none." Abner nodded to himself.

I wasn't worried in the slightest. I didn't even know I had a functioning greenhouse, having not had the time to explore the little building, barely giving it a cursory glance or two since moving in a few months back.

"But, Abner, as much as I get a little thrill rush through me, every time I see your face—or hear your voice—what are you doing here? In my kitchen? Don't you have a home somewhere nearby or something you need to worry about?" Or heaven forbid! A wife? And that thrill coursing in my veins had more to do with thoughts of murder than any other emotion I might be experiencing.

Abner, however, ignorant of this, looked pleased and a bit

touched by my concern. I wasn't about to correct his assumptions.

"Lily, Abner lives here on the property. I told you he is our handyman. He has been for years! He lives in that tiny cabin behind the greenhouse."

There is a tiny cabin behind the greenhouse?

"Can't see it for the kudzu growing over it. But I like it the same. Exceptin' when the weather gets this cold. With all my handymanin' and gardenin' I plumb forgot to chop any firewood last Autumn. Now, well, the place gets cold, and my heater is on its last legs."

I looked over to Lorcan, who seemed as shocked at this news as I was.

"Abner! You should have told me. I would have brought you some. We can take care of it today." I loved Lorcan for his big heart, and the rest of the town wasn't too far behind me.

I sighed inwardly and continued, "Let me know what kind of heater you need, Abner, and I will get one and have it installed. In the meantime, I guess you can stay here."

I did not just say that.

"Oh! No, no. Got some windows to fix over at Lorcan's shop, and I'm gonna spend the day there. Then this evening, I have my poker group. Not even an ice storm can stop us from meeting! Gordy said I could spend the night, so I'm good."

You might be Abner, but did anyone inform Sheila? I had a feeling Gordy was about to be in the doghouse. Or not. I mean, Abner does have some sort of appeal. If you like Captain Obvious one-liners, that grate on your last nerve.

"Plus, Stu is stayin' over and he's the one givin' me the ride to Gordy and Sheila's. She put on a big pot of beef stew for us and is stayin' out of our way. I heard she's with Shirley tonight and they're playing the Bunco. Shirley has troubles, and Sheila is tryin' to distract her."

I think it's just Bunco, but what did I know?

Stu is a part-time mechanic that works for Lorcan. He's Sheila and Shirley's little brother. A sweet guy if a bit slow, but he's another man in this town with a good heart. You just had to wait two weeks for him to come up with the right words to finish one sentence.

He's also our mayor.

Shocking. I know.

Small Georgia towns. Gotta love them.

"Is Shirley well? Is there anything we can do?" I asked, hoping it wasn't a serious matter as I already felt stretched thin with my own troubles.

"Don't rightly know. Gordy and Sheila didn't say."

Sheila worked at Joe's Diner, my favorite food place in all Sweet Briar. Shirley, her big sister, was the town's EMT.

"Ok, then. Can I ask why then we have this little impromptu breakfast going on during an ice storm? Minus Abner being here?"

"Because I'm hungry, and you have a stocked fridge."

Ack!

I spun around to see the diminutive form of my great-grandmother, Adriana Dolce, standing behind me looking smug in her grey wool shawl covering her pajamas with fuzzy green slippers on her feet. Pajamas?

"Were you here all night? When did you get here? I'm confused." I said as I walked over to my chair and motioned Abner to get out of it. He did, grabbing his plate and almost absconding with my mug, but I was too quick for him.

I went to the sink, rinsed it, then poured myself a cup—black, like my mood—and stomped into the den where I curled up in my favorite chair.

Adelaide frowned at me as she handed a grateful Abner

another mug of coffee. He nodded and grinned in appreciation.

Adriana continued. "I spent the night, and you'd know this if you hadn't have gone to bed at seven like a toddler."

"For your information, there is a winter storm going on, and I was up the previous night making sure we had candles and supplies while the lights kept flickering. I was waiting for a tree to come crashing through my roof with all that wind we had, and I am sleep-deprived. That still doesn't explain how you got here and when!"

"I've been here since Thursday." Adriana sniffed.

It was Saturday.

"I don't even." I took a sip of my coffee, grimaced, and stomped back into the kitchen, where I doctored my brew with heaps of sugar and cream.

"If you must know, my car broke down on Wednesday, and I had it towed to your lover boy's place. I spent the night at June's then came here by foot. You locked your door so that I couldn't get in, but Wicked saw me looking in your back door and opened it for me."

I glared at my cat, who seemed amused by the interplay. Don't ask how Wicked managed to open a locked door. I have given up trying to figure it out.

"I called Keisha and informed her I'd not be home until the storm let up and just caught her before she left for the day. She locked the house up, making sure she'd turned my heat up, so my pipes don't freeze. Then she made it safely back to her place because I checked in on her. So, with no pressing matters to attend to at home, I decided I'd stay here."

Wait. No pressing... "How can you say that? What about Grandfather Antonio? You can't just leave him alone with no one to care for him! How can you be so cruel?!" I was shocked that my great-grandmother would be so inconsiderate and downright negligible. Keisha, too, since she was his nurse and all.

"Oh, he'll be fine. Or not. Either he will be warm and toasty, or the heat will fail, and he will freeze to death." Adriana said this with a gleam of amusement in her eyes, causing me to grasp I was being trifled with. She was obviously joking, I think.

I kept staring at her until she finally rolled her eyes so hard, teenagers around the world became envious.

"Ok, fine. You big baby. He's at his cabin in the woods near Pot Gap Ridge near Dick's Knob."

Did you understand any of that? I was afraid even to ask.

"Why is he alone in a cabin in the woods, on the top of a mountain, during an ice storm?" I asked, fearing the answer would be something beyond my scope of comprehension.

Adriana waltzed into the kitchen, grabbed a handful of bacon, and began to consume it loudly.

"Who said he was alone? Mortimer is with him."

Mortimer was a vampire. This should make any sane person quake, but I am no sane person. Especially since finding out I was a witch and came from a crackpot family of witches. All of them crazy, and most of them within thirty square miles of the town of Sweet Briar, Georgia, where I now lived.

Long story short, I was born here. I left with my aunt, who I thought was my mother at the time, lived for years in the upstate of New York, in the Catskill Mountains, then upon her death, returned "home" to Sweet Briar per her instructions. Only to find out I come from a dynasty of witches, some of whom are dark—and in Adriana's case, pure evil.

Ok, so I am a dark witch as well.

Please don't hold it against me. It does not mean we are malevolent or do horrible acts with bubbling cauldrons at the ready. It means we battle dark forces with our unique ability to control dark magic.

Despite my ignorance of all things witch, growing up, I've quickly caught up and think I am getting rather proficient at spellcasting, if I may say so!

Mortimer is a friendly vampire whose parents have retired and live in a retirement condo village in Florida.

I know, I know.

Who knew vampires would ever retire and move to the Sunshine State? Apparently, the older a vampire got, they became less affected by the sun. I guess it didn't hurt that he was part shifter as well.

Believe me. I am still trying to get a handle on the paranormal world myself, having grown up a human.

"Why is Mortimer with Antonio? And now? With the weather this bad?"

Sighing in exasperation, Adriana picked up her coffee and downed it in one gulp, then slammed the mug on the counter.

"Because they are tracking the new warden of the prison so they can find out the secret entrance, sneak in, then transport me there. This way, I can finally get answers from Donna Fredricks before I choke the life out of her. Or die trying."

And that's how my weekend started, folks! Little did I know how much worse it was about to get.

SOCIAL MEDIA LINKS

I write in my own style that may not be everyone's cup of tea —so if you enjoy my characters and humor, my plots, how the storyline is developing, etc. and are eagerly anticipating the next in the series, be aware that I am just as excited as you are—I've found someone who thinks my story ideas are neat! That is thrilling for any writer to know (or it should be). THANK YOU!

Visit my official website to receive updates, find out about special offers and new releases, or read my blog about writing and farm life - complete with photos - you might even catch me mowing my ten acres (seriously): http://www.bettinamjohnson.net

For more information or to contact me:
author@bettinamjohnson.net

For even more (if you just can't enough of me) follow my Social Media Links

Mailing List - https://bit.ly/2BvQXmP
BookBub - https://bit.ly/2Epejwj
Goodreads - https://bit.ly/3aTejQW
Author Page - Amazon - https://amzn.to/3lj7L2L
Instagram - https://bit.ly/2QpZa01
TikTok - https://bit.ly/2PQa6Hg
MeWe - https://bit.ly/36A2RcM
Facebook - https://bit.ly/3gOaFZY
Twitter: https://bit.ly/3jahMgY
YouTube - https://bit.ly/2Stvy2X

ABOUT THE AUTHOR

I always knew I wanted to write. As a kid, way before the technology age had hit, I'd be stuck in the car with the folks as we drove from our home on Staten Island, NY, where I was born and raised, to our family property in the Catskill Mountains. To drive away boredom, I would sit, staring out the window, and create adventures of daring thieves riding horseback along the road, trying to escape the law. Other times I'd imagine a wild girl riding her unicorn into battle (I had a vivid imagination - we didn't have video games yet!).

As the years passed, I'd start writing a book, then stop, then start again only to let life get in the way, until one day I had an epiphany—a kick in the pants moment. If I waited any longer, all those wonderful characters in my head would never have their stories told, and that made me sad. So, I treated writing as my career. Once I started, it became apparent nothing would ever stop me again. YOU, dear reader, are stuck with me until I go off to that great library in the sky...or wherever writers go when they crumble to dust in front of their typewriters (or laptops...whatever!).

I live in the North Georgia mountains on what I like to call a farm, with my husband and almost adult kids, a Cairn Terrier, a bunch of cats, and fish. Occasionally other critters show up to keep things exciting.

BOOKS BY BETTINA M. JOHNSON

The Lily Sweet Mysteries:

Home Sweet Witch

Witch Way is Up?

How To Train Your Witch

Sweet Home Liliana

Witch Way Did He Go?

Revenge is Sweet, Witch

Witch and Peace

The Sweet Spell of Success (Coming Soon)

* * *

The Fortune-Telling Twins Mysteries:

A Tale of Two Sisters

Double Toil and Trouble

Fire and Earth, Sisters at Birth (Coming Soon)